The
Dashwood
Sisters
tell all

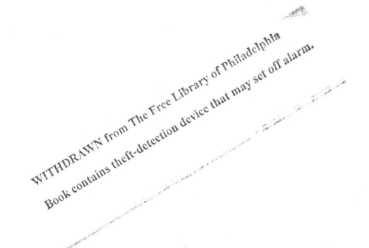

The
Dashwood Sisters
tell all

A MODERN-DAY NOVEL OF JANE AUSTEN

BETH PATTILLO

Guideposts
New York, New York

The Dashwood Sisters Tell All

ISBN-10: 0-8249-4874-2
ISBN-13: 978-0-8249-4874-0

Published by Guideposts
16 East 34th Street
New York, New York 10016
www.guideposts.org

Distributed by Ideals Publications, a Guideposts company
2630 Elm Hill Pike, Suite 100
Nashville, TN 37214

Guideposts and *Ideals* are registered trademarks of Guideposts.

The characters and events in this book are fictional, and any resemblance to
actual persons or events is coincidental.

Library of Congress Cataloging-in-Publication Data

Pattillo, Beth.
  The Dashwood sisters tell all / by Beth Pattillo.
    p. cm.
  ISBN-13: 978-0-8249-4874-0
  ISBN-10: 0-8249-4874-2
  1. Austen, Jane, 1775–1817—Appreciation—Fiction.   2. Sisters—Fiction.
  3. Literary landmarks–Fiction.   4. England–Fiction.   I. Title.

  PS3616.A925D37   2011
  813′.6–dc22   2010043782

Cover design by Georgia Morrissey
Cover art by Trevillion Images
Interior design by Lorie Pagnozzi
Map by Rose Lowry www.illustrations.com
Typeset by Aptara

Printed and bound in the United States of America
10 9 8 7 6 5 4 3 2 1

FOR MY FELLOW WAYFARERS . . .
BOB AND CLAIRE, NANCY, OKSANNA, GRETA,
HAL AND BARBARA, JOYCE, AND BARBARA W., AND
FOR PHILLIPPA, OUR FEARLESS LEADER, AND
YANNICK, OUR INTREPID MANAGER,
THANKS FOR A LOVELY RAMBLE
THROUGH HAMPSHIRE.

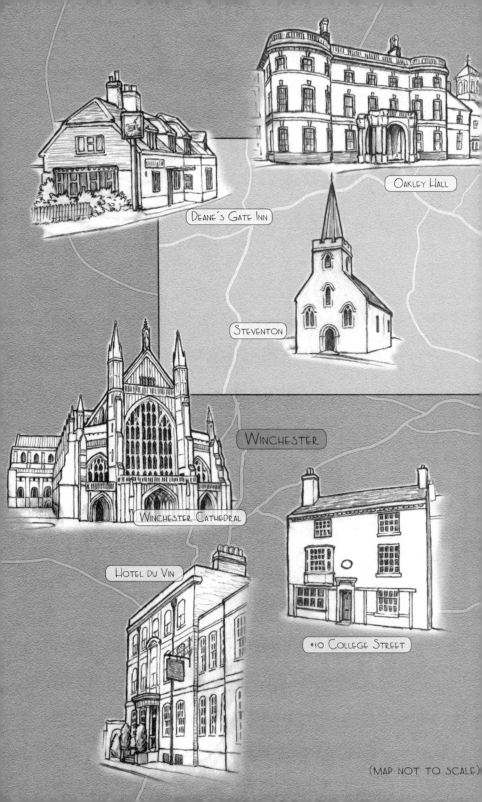

Oakley Hall

Deane's Gate Inn

Steventon

Winchester

Winchester Cathedral

Hotel du Vin

*10 College Street

(MAP NOT TO SCALE)

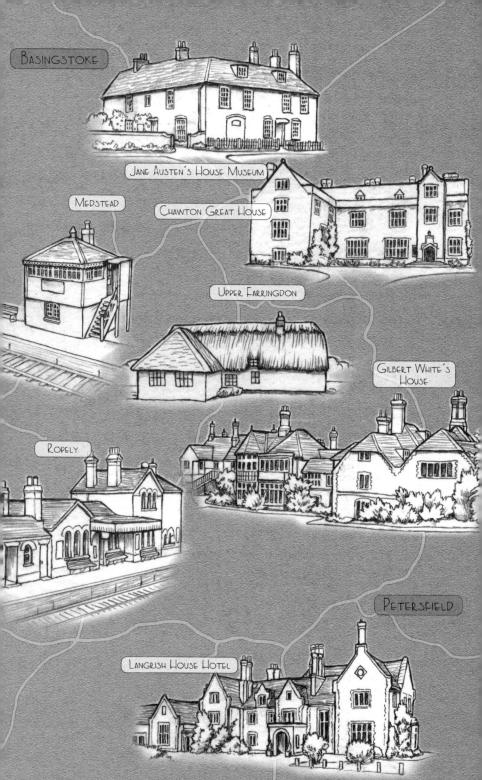

BASINGSTOKE

JANE AUSTEN'S HOUSE MUSEUM

MEDSTEAD

CHAWTON GREAT HOUSE

UPPER FARRINGDON

GILBERT WHITE'S HOUSE

ROPELY

PETERSFIELD

LANGRISH HOUSE HOTEL

should never have agreed to travel with my sister, even if my mother's will required it. Yet there I stood on the driveway of Oakley Hall in Hampshire on a warm June day, watching Mimi drag her suitcase the last few steps to the entrance of the country house hotel.

"Please, Ellen," Mimi pleaded. She paused to force the wheels of her suitcase through the gravel.

"I told you before we left that you had to carry your own luggage." I knew if I didn't stand firm, I would be toting her Louis Vuitton monstrosity around for the rest of the week.

"I thought there would be bellmen. This is England. Didn't they invent civilization?" She pushed a blonde, spiral curl out of her eyes.

"Actually, it was the Greeks who invented civilization."

"Well, then, I bet the Greeks have bellmen."

We'd missed the minibus from the tour company that was supposed to give us a ride from the train station at Basingstoke to Oakley Hall, the start of our walking tour. The hotel was like something out of a BBC costume drama, with its three stories of red brick, numerous white-sashed windows, and elegant marble columns and pediment above the entrance.

"I'm sorry we missed the bus, okay?" Mimi drooped to a stop beside me. "I thought I had time for a facial before we left London."

She didn't need a facial, of course. Her skin was almost as dewy perfect now as it had been when she was five. But my sister would never have believed me if I told her that, no matter how solemnly I swore.

"At least we're here," I said. "We'd better see about checking in." I picked up my carry-on.

"I can't believe that's all you brought." Mimi eyed my small suitcase with a mixture of envy and frustration.

"I've got a tote bag too." I hitched its handles higher on my shoulder.

"I still don't understand why we have to do this." Mimi gave her suitcase another fruitless tug. "Why couldn't Mom just make a normal will like other people's parents?"

I snorted. "We *are* talking about Caroline Dodge."

Our mother had been the most Jane Austen–obsessed person I had ever known. I'd always thought it was because she was British. After she met and married my American dad, he dragged her back to the States to the land of suburbs and minivans and fast-food drive-throughs. She'd never quite gotten over the culture shock.

"Is what she wanted even legal?" Mimi looked dubious. "Can you just sprinkle someone's ashes in Hampshire without permission?"

"If you don't get caught." I hoped I sounded more certain than I felt.

"What if we can't pull it off?" Mimi voiced my biggest fear. My mother's will had been very clear. Both of us must participate in this Jane Austen–themed walking tour in Hampshire, and we must agree on the most appropriate place to scatter her ashes. Once that happened, we could contact her lawyer, and he would release our inheritance to us.

I didn't actually care all that much about the money, although it would certainly come in handy. I knew why my mother had made this last, quirky request. She thought that giving us this assignment would finally make Mimi and me bond as sisters. I could have told her it was useless and saved a bundle on plane fares. But when your mother is dying, you tend to go along with whatever she wants, even if you have to go to another continent to do it.

The front door of Oakley Hall swung open, and a man appeared. Tall, fifty-something, good-looking in a mature way, with a sun-browned face and threads of gray in his hair. He strode toward us with an unmistakable military bearing, and I liked him on sight. He looked dependable, a characteristic that had been missing in a lot of the men I had known.

He came to a stop in front of us. "Good afternoon, ladies." He had an American accent. "You must be the Dodge sisters." He extended his hand to me. "I'm Tom Braddock, the tour leader."

I shook his hand. "I'm Ellen. This is my sister, Mimi."

He reached over and picked up Mimi's suitcase with masculine confidence. "Let me help you with this."

I had learned early on in life not to wait around for a man's help, so I fell into step behind Tom, carrying my own luggage.

"How many people are in the group?" I asked as we made our way through the front door of Oakley Hall and into the reception room.

"We're expecting ten," Tom said over his shoulder. He escorted us to the front desk. A young woman with a sleek bun and a chic black jacket stood on the other side, a phone pressed to her ear.

"Ten plus you," Mimi said to Tom, flirting with him automatically. She really couldn't help herself. I knew that. The knowledge didn't make it any easier to watch though. I thought that Tom Braddock might have actually blushed.

"Yes. Ten plus myself," he said. "An old friend of mine owns the tour company. I retired early last year and took this up as a sideline."

"Retired?" Mimi's smile wilted.

I hid my own smile. The greatest fear of any beauty is aging, and Mimi was no exception.

"United States Air Force. I spent several years stationed here and decided to come back."

"You must have traveled a lot," I said. It sounded adventurous and romantic. I'd spent my whole life in Dallas, except for the occasional family vacation to the Gulf Coast. When I was young, my mother couldn't convince my father to take her back to England to visit. When I was older, after my father was gone, she seemed to have lost the desire to see her homeland.

I wanted to ask Tom about his travels, but Mimi's attention had already wandered. She gazed around the reception room, admiring the tall ceilings, the intricate moldings, and the general air of elegance. Tom's smile sagged a bit, but I tamped down any feelings of sympathy. I was tired of binding up the romantic wounds my sister inflicted or suffered. I had enough problems of my own to deal with at the moment.

The young woman behind the reception desk put down the receiver and turned her attention to us. "How may I help you?"

I took care of checking us in while Mimi looked on. We might be well into our thirties, but somehow we'd never outgrown our childhood roles. I took care of the details while Mimi brought the enthusiasm. I provided the sense, as my mother used to say, and Mimi provided the sensibility. Just like in the Austen novel. She'd even given us names similar to the famous Dashwood sisters.

At least my mother had shown enough foresight to book the pair of us into separate rooms for the duration of our trip.

"Ellen?"

I turned to find Mimi frowning at me. "What's the matter?"

"What if this doesn't work out?"

The deep lines around her mouth told me that she was very worried about that possibility. "It'll be fine, Meems. We'll figure it out."

She looked doubtful.

"It's going to be okay," I said, but without much conviction. "Let's go find our rooms."

⚜⚜⚜⚜⚜

Once Ellen checked us in, I finally got that bellman I'd been wishing for. I couldn't keep flirting with the tour leader just so he'd haul my suitcase around. Even I knew there were limits. Besides, Tom Braddock didn't need any more encouragement from me. He seemed nice enough, but he was way too old and stodgy. I had enough people in my life already who disapproved of everything I did. I didn't need to add one more.

Although that number had recently decreased by one when my mother died.

The bellman told me he'd meet me at my room, which wasn't in the main house at all but was out in the stable block. He said something about getting a cart, and I could only hope the rooms weren't too far away. My high heels were killing me. Ellen had practically gone purple when I'd turned up in them that morning in the lobby of our hotel, but I wasn't about to be seen in London in sensible shoes like my sister was wearing.

The woman behind the desk directed us through the main part of the hotel and out a rear terrace door. From there, another crushed-shell walk led to the stable block. As I wobbled my way across the shells, I was doubly thankful for the bellman. I'd never have gotten King Louis, as Ellen called my suitcase, over this terrain.

I rounded the stable block and found myself in its courtyard. It was paved with red brick that matched the building, and the wood trim and doors of the stable block were painted a sparkling white. Very tidy, if a bit spare. I held my key card up to the sensor by the door, and the lock clicked open.

The room was absolute heaven. It was huge, for one thing, and decorated in neutrals, with crisp white walls. The bathroom was enormous by English hotel standards, and the luxurious tray of toiletries even included a rubber duck for the bath.

I kicked off my torturous shoes and flopped down on the pristine white duvet. I could gladly spend the week right here in this room rather than stalking around the countryside.

I didn't want to deal with my mother's ashes. Thankfully Ellen had agreed to carry the box around. I'd struggled enough just going back to Dallas for the funeral. That should have been the end of it, but obviously my mother had other ideas.

My mother had always had other ideas.

The bellman brought my suitcase into the room. It took me a moment to figure out the coins so I could tip him the right amount. I felt like a first grader all over again, trying to remember which coins were which. It didn't help that in

England the ten-pence pieces were the size of nickels, and the five-pence pieces were the size of dimes.

After the bellman left, I wanted to fling myself on the bed again, but I needed to unpack before my clothes got any more wrinkled. We had a welcome reception and dinner in a matter of hours, and I needed all the time I could get to pull myself together.

I emptied my carry-on and tossed the copy of *Sense and Sensibility* I'd brought with me on the nightstand. My mother had always been after me to read it. I'd compromised by seeing the movie, but after she got sick, I'd had a change of heart and bought the book. I had known that my mother fancied Ellen and me as some modern-day version of the Dashwood sisters, but that was all it had been. A fancy. We were just too different. I was too spontaneous, too inclined to live in the moment for Ellen to take me seriously. And she was far too dull for me to want to spend any more time with her than necessary.

I eyed the small amount of hanging space in the wardrobe. The English really needed to work on their closets. No way were all my dresses going to fit, much less any of the hiking clothes Ellen insisted that I bring.

I sighed and contemplated the drawer space in the built-in unit next to the wardrobe. Whatever happened during the coming week, I would do whatever it took to meet the terms of my mother's will. I was going to get my hands on my inheritance.

My college friend Stacey, a real-estate agent in New York City, had found the perfect space in SoHo for my boutique, but I had to come up with a deposit, and fast. I was so close to my dream coming true, to leaving Atlanta behind and finally making it to the center of the fashion world.

The knock at the door startled me. I scooped up my lingerie and shoved it into a drawer. When I opened the door, I wasn't surprised to find Tom, the tour leader, standing there.

"Sorry to disturb you," he began.

I opened my mouth to say something dismissive. I'd learned early on that persistent men usually needed to be told in no uncertain terms to buzz off. But then I saw the handbag he was holding. My handbag, which I must have set down in the lobby and then walked off and left.

"Thank you!" I seized it and hugged it to my chest. It wasn't real Chanel, but only a very discerning eye could tell the difference. "I appreciate you bringing it to me."

"You're welcome. I had a feeling you might miss it." He smiled, and it really did make him look younger.

"You're an angel. Thank you." I was relieved that I'd misjudged him. He seemed like a nice guy. Maybe we could be friends.

"No problem. I'll see you at the welcome dinner. Drinks at seven in the library."

"Wouldn't miss it." I gave him another smile, and he waved as he walked away.

Then I was alone again. It felt strangely . . . well . . . lonely.

I looked around the empty room and sighed. A small part of me wished that my mother had booked Ellen and me into the same room. We were a long way from home, after all. We didn't know anyone else on the tour, and Ellen was all the family I had left.

For whatever that was worth to either of us now.

sent Mimi on ahead with the first bellman and waited for my own, who escorted me to my room in the stable block. It didn't take long to unpack my few things and hang my bag of toiletries in the bathroom. I opened my tote bag and took out the large brown envelope I'd received in the mail a few days before I flew to England.

The envelope was from my mother's attorneys. Even before it arrived in the mail, I'd received a call from her lawyer, instructing me not to open it until I arrived at Oakley Hall.

"Your mother would like for you and your sister to decide what to do with this item," he'd said.

"I don't understand. What kind of item?"

"She said that you would understand once you opened it."

It wasn't like my mother to be cryptic. I turned the envelope over in my hands, a potential Pandora's box. I'd followed the instructions, but I hadn't been above feeling the envelope to figure out what was inside—a flat, rectangular object. My guess was a book, but given my mother's elaborate plans for this tour and the scattering of her ashes, I wouldn't bet money on it.

The weight of the package in my hands was a physical reminder of the weight I'd been carrying on my shoulders for months. The walls of the hotel room suddenly felt as if they were closing in on me. What I really needed was fresh air. I shoved the envelope back in my tote, slung it over my shoulder, and left my room.

Instead of returning to the main part of the hotel, I followed the path that led in the opposite direction, toward a small cottage that peeked through the trees. I'd find a shady spot and just sit, away from sisters and wills and mysterious packages. I knew my mother had meant well, sending Mimi and me on this trip together, but she couldn't really have imagined that it would help. By Friday, the two of us would no doubt be even more at odds with each other than we usually were.

I walked briskly, and a few hundred yards along the path, I was already out of breath. How in the world would I survive a whole week of walking? Once upon a time, I'd been in good shape. But that had been before time and career and family demands took their toll. I'd meant to start exercising months ago to get in shape, but per usual, other things had gotten in the way.

I looked up and saw a man coming toward me on the path. He was about my height and age, with dark hair. I resisted the urge to smooth my own windblown mop. The last thing I needed to worry about on this trip was how I looked. As the man came closer, I could see his face more clearly. I stumbled and then righted myself and kept moving, but my heart exploded into a loud hammering in my chest. It couldn't be. It was impossible. It was . . .

My first impulse was to turn around and make a run for Oakley Hall. Instead, I forced myself to keep breathing and moving toward him. His presence made no sense. I hadn't seen him for more than fifteen years. Not since college graduation. Not since we'd said good-bye and he'd walked away with his fiancée on his arm.

We were thirty feet apart now, and I saw it in his face the moment he realized who I was. Part of me wanted to smile at this unexpected meeting with an old friend, because he was that, if nothing else. But another part of me wanted to weep. I was dealing with enough new losses already. I didn't need to be reminded of this one too.

When he was ten feet away, I forced myself to smile. "Hello, Daniel."

He grinned. "Of all the forests in all the counties in all of England . . . " He shook his head. "I can't believe it's you."

"Me, neither." I didn't know whether to stick out my hand for him to shake or to give him an awkward hug. Neither seemed right. "What are you doing here?"

He laughed, a familiar and somehow comforting sound. Years might have passed, but he still had the same good-natured, warm laugh. "I could ask you the same thing."

"Obviously you're staying at Oakley Hall," I said. He stepped forward, until we were a mere two feet apart. "Wait. You aren't on the Jane Austen tour, are you?" My stomach dropped to my ankles.

"Actually, yes."

Panic exploded in my chest. "But, why . . . I mean, Jane Austen? You?" He'd been a business major, and the few announcements I'd seen in the alumni magazine had charted the course of his successful career as an international antiques dealer. After a few years, I'd quit reading the alumni magazine. "I thought you were more of a John Steinbeck kind of guy."

"I was. I mean, I am."

"So you're here under spousal duress?" I refused to let my panic show on my face.

"No. I'm here alone." He flexed his left hand at his side, and that was when I noticed he wasn't wearing a wedding ring. "Melissa and I . . . well, we're not together anymore."

The thrill that went through me at the knowledge was wrong. Of course it was. But that didn't do anything to discourage it.

He looked at me then, really looked at me. Our gazes met, and suddenly I wasn't thirty-eight but eighteen, meeting him for the first time at freshman orientation. My life had changed in that one moment. Irrevocably. Permanently. Eternally. And then Melissa had stepped up next to him, and he'd introduced me to his high-school sweetheart. They'd decided on colleges together, she'd said. They were planning to get married as soon as they graduated. And I had settled for friendship for the next four years.

He stepped forward and caught my arm. "Are you okay? You look like you've seen a ghost." I didn't object when he led me to an enormous fallen log. "Sit down," he said. "Should I get you some water?"

"No. I'm fine." I tried to breathe deeply, and after a moment my head cleared and I felt normal again. "It's just been quite a day."

"Do you want to tell me about it?"

"It's a long story."

He lowered himself to the log beside me and stretched out his legs. "I have as long as you need. Unless you'd rather be alone."

How in the world had all this happened? How had I come to be sitting on a log in the middle of England with the one man I'd ever loved?

"No, I'm fine. Just surprised to see you."

He was silent for a long moment. I would have expected some forest rustlings, some birdsong from the trees above, but the world was still and quiet. And then I heard it, a lone bird with a rather plaintive cry. *Too late. Too late*, it seemed to say.

"Daniel—"

"Ellen—"

We spoke at the same time and then stopped. Then we laughed, although my reaction was more from nerves than humor.

"This can't be a coincidence," I said. "I think I detect the hand of my mother in all of this." Why else would Daniel have turned up on a Jane Austen walking tour?

"You would be right," he said with a rueful smile, "but maybe not for the reasons you think."

"Oh?" My cheeks went flame red. Was I that transparent?

"Your mom contacted me before she . . . passed away. She said she wanted to hire me to come on this trip."

"Hire you?" Confusion tightened my chest. "I don't understand." Most likely my mother had concocted some elaborate cover story just to get him to Hampshire, where she hoped I might finally catch the man of my dreams. How in the world had she known about his divorce?

"In my professional capacity. She said you were coming here to dispose of a family heirloom. When she told me about her . . . situation"—he paused—"well, I couldn't say no."

Of course he couldn't. He might have broken my heart, but he was a decent man who would want to do the right thing, especially when the request came from the dying mother of an old friend.

"Daniel, I'm sorry she troubled you—"

"I'm not." He bumped his shoulder gently against mine, as though we were kids sitting in the schoolyard at recess. "I was glad for the chance to see you again."

The thrill that shot up my spine at his words scared me. I'd spent the better part of two decades getting over this man, and now my mother had reached out from the grave to set me up for heartbreak all over again. Because I had a strong suspicion that whatever this "family heirloom" might be, it was just an excuse for her to finagle a second chance at love for me.

"So, what is this priceless artifact?" he asked. "Jewelry? A portrait?"

"Actually, I have no idea."

Daniel gave me a funny look. "Do you have it with you? I mean, is it here? In England?"

I pulled the envelope from my tote bag. "Right here. But the lawyer said my mother's instructions were not to open it until I got here."

Daniel scooted closer. "Well, let's see what we're dealing with."

I pulled the tab on the envelope and slid out the contents—a book of some sort, covered in bubble wrap. I unwound the plastic as Daniel watched. The book was old, the leather scuffed and darkened to a mottled mahogany. I flipped it open, but instead of printed letters, I saw old-fashioned handwriting.

"It's a diary of some sort," I said to Daniel.

I flipped to the front, wondering if it had been my mother's. But it wasn't her writing, and I quickly discovered that whatever my mother had hoped Mimi and I would do with this diary, there wasn't any chance of returning it to the original owner.

On the flyleaf, the author had written . . .

Private Property of Miss Cassandra Austen.

Do Not Read.

That Means You, Jane.

llen would be proud of me. For once I was on time to a social event. My beauty routine usually put me in the "fashionably late" crowd, but that evening I entered the library of Oakley Hall along with most of the guests. Ahead of my sister, even.

Tom Braddock was there by the drinks table, looking crisp in a green pin-striped oxford shirt and a pressed pair of khakis. I thought again that it was too bad he was so old. He had some very appealing qualities.

"Festive or sensible?" he asked with a smile.

I wrinkled my nose. "Festive. Sensible is Ellen's department."

He chuckled in response and gallantly presented me with a champagne flute.

The library was beautiful—the long rectangular room boasted a thick blue carpet, yellow and white period-style furniture, gold chandeliers, and handsome wood paneling that framed shelf after shelf of books. The window at the far end of the room overlooked the terrace. Beyond it, the lawn led off into woods, with fields in the distance.

"It's amazing. Like something out of a ... well ... an Austen novel," I said to Tom.

"We thought the tour participants would like it."

I studied him for a moment. "So you planned the tour?"

He shook his head. "It was a special request, but once the company put it up on the Web site, it filled up fast." He set his empty glass on a nearby table. "Would you like to meet some of your fellow walkers?"

"Of course."

I met Carol and Ralph, a nice couple from Nashville, and a couple from Nebraska, who seemed very kind. Karen, from New York, was a television producer. Charlotte was a retired lawyer from LA. And there were a few others whose names I couldn't remember. Ellen and I were clearly the youngest in the group. I'd been hoping for at least one single man, just to keep me on top of my game, but I knew in my heart of hearts that the only men likely to turn up on a Jane Austen walking tour would be either husbands pressed into service by their wives or men who were probably as interested in finding a real-life Mr. Darcy as I was.

"And here's the last member of the group. Besides your sister," Tom said. I turned, and then I had to make a conscious effort not to let my mouth hang open.

"This is Ethan Blakemore," Tom said. "Ethan, this is Mimi Dodge."

The man wasn't simply gorgeous. He was drop-dead gorgeous. He was also about my age and wearing a very expensive silk shirt and well-tailored trousers. I dared a brief glimpse at his shoes. Italian loafers.

Come to Mama.

"A pleasure to meet you," Ethan said in a posh British accent that made my mouth water. Then he took my hand. At first I thought he was actually going to kiss it, but instead he gently squeezed my fingers in a courtly gesture that was far more enticing than a handshake.

"Nice to meet you too." Well, that wasn't very original. But from the way he was looking at me, I wouldn't have to be original. I'd suspected that the strapless, pink dress was overkill, but now I was glad I'd gone the extra mile.

"You're from America." Ethan reached out and gently took my arm. "Which part?" Before I could put together a coherent reply, he'd neatly turned me away from Tom and the rest of the group. I wasn't about to resist.

"I'm originally from Dallas, but I've been living in Atlanta." I wish I could have said New York or Los Angeles. Atlanta sounded so provincial. "What about you?"

Ethan smiled, which revealed brilliantly white teeth. "I live in London, but I recently inherited a property here in Hampshire."

Which meant he had some money, most likely. I knew I couldn't just come right out and ask him what he did for a living. "Did you grow up in London?"

He nodded. "A city boy, I'm afraid."

"And you're an Austen fan?" There had to be a catch.

"Well . . . " He looked over his shoulder, like a naughty schoolboy, and leaned in to whisper his answer. "Perhaps I should say that I'm an admirer of the women who admire Jane Austen."

Color rose in my cheeks, and I resisted the urge to fan myself with my hand. I decided I might just forgive my mother for forcing Ellen and me into this charade after all.

"That's always nice to hear," I said with what I hoped was the right mixture of dignity and flirtatiousness. I'd learned years ago that British men were tricky to flirt with. They thought American women possessed universally loose morals, but they didn't want the girls from across the pond to be too forward or cheeky. It was a delicate balance.

Ethan guided me into the far corner of the room. I tried not to let his obvious attentions go to my head. After all, I was the only woman under fifty in view.

"So you routinely go on walking tours to meet women?" I said with a little laugh. "I wouldn't think you'd have a lot of difficulty in that department."

"It's not a question of meeting women. It's a question of meeting the right women."

I would rather he'd used the singular than the plural, but I could applaud the sentiment.

"If you have a house here, I'm surprised you haven't done all this Jane Austen stuff before."

"I have. Bits of it, anyway. But the idea of walking the footpaths interested me."

"Not just the Austenites then?"

He laughed and then drained his glass. "The house I've inherited came to my mother through the Austens. My mother married into the extended family late in life. I decided to take the tour to find out what all the fuss was about. It was obviously an excellent decision." He smiled at me in a way that was surely designed to leave me weak in the knees. And it did.

Warmth rose from my midsection, up to my shoulders and throat, and then into a thick fog that engulfed my head. I'd been so busy being angry at my mother for making me come on this trip that I hadn't given it a real chance. Ethan offered to get me another drink, and I decided that, really, it would only be sporting to try and enjoy myself. My mother might have sent Ellen and me on a rather morbid errand, but it looked as if there might be some compensation in store in the form of one genuine Austen-issue hero.

❦❦❦❦❦

Mimi was the one who was always late, not me. Yet here I was, hurrying from the stable block to the welcome reception more than fifteen minutes behind schedule. I felt I should be forgiven for my lateness, though, given the bombshell that had been dropped in my lap. What had my mother been thinking?

The diary couldn't be real, of course. In all the years I'd listened to my mother ramble on about all things Austen, I'd never heard any mention of Jane Austen's only sister keeping a diary. I suspected it must be a fake, but Daniel hadn't been as convinced of that as I was.

"We'll need to have it authenticated," he'd said. "No wonder your mom wanted me to come on this tour." He hadn't asked to touch or hold the diary but had been content to peek over my shoulder while I did. "I don't have a lot of contacts in England, but I can make some calls."

"It can't be real, Dan." Couldn't he see that it was bait? Daniel bait?

"Your mother never struck me as someone who would lie about something like this."

"I know." That troubled me. The hopeless romantic part of my mother might have stooped to a little trickery in the name of true love, but the Jane Austen devotee in her wouldn't have been inclined to manufacture a fake diary and sign Cassandra's name to it.

Before we returned to the hotel, Daniel had agreed not to mention the diary to anyone until I told him he could. The first person I needed to talk to was Mimi, of course. Maybe she knew something about this mysterious family heirloom, although I doubted it. She was so eager to get her hands on our inheritance for whatever business proposition she had up her proverbial and fashionable sleeve. If she possessed any knowledge of an authentic, priceless Austen artifact in the family, she would have sprinted to the nearest auction house.

And now that diary had made me late to the welcome reception. I picked my way across the crushed-shell walk between the stable block and the main building, and then dashed across the terrace. A set of French doors stood open to the waning afternoon, so I ducked inside, crossed through a conference room, skirted my way around the edge of the bar, and stepped into the library.

I paused just inside the door to catch my breath and smooth the skirt of my sensible blue shirtwaist dress. My efforts didn't remove the suitcase-induced wrinkles. I should have stayed safely in my room, ironing, instead of opening mysterious packages and fanning old flames. My throat was dry, but I couldn't tell if it was from summer pollen or simply from nerves.

I plucked a glass of champagne from the tray on a nearby table. My hand shook, but I was afraid to hold the glass too tightly. The last thing I needed was for the stem to snap. I'd spent my life not calling attention to myself. A champagne glass shattering in my hand was definitely not my style.

I declined the offer of a shrimp puff from a server and forced myself to sip, rather than gulp, my drink. Composure was a matter of rising above one's circumstances. At least that's what my mother had always said. I'd believed her and made that my mantra. It's just that I never would have imagined having to follow her advice after she'd dumped a priceless Austen heirloom on me.

"There you are." Mimi appeared beside me in a strapless, rosy confection that showed off her lightly tanned shoulders. She twirled her glass between her fingers as she surveyed the room, perfectly at ease. "You have to come meet Ethan."

"Who's Ethan?" The glow in her cheeks came from something other than Elizabeth Arden.

"He's a yummy singleton from London who's related to Jane Austen."

The sparkle was back in her eyes, but I had learned long ago to be wary of it. "Is he on the tour?"

Mimi smiled. "That's the best part. C'mon."

She grabbed my hand and towed me across the room, but before we could reach her latest quarry, an older woman with vibrantly orange hair stepped in front of us.

"You must be the Dodge sisters." Despite the warmth of the June day, she wore a tweed suit that was neither brown nor gray but some unfortunate hybrid of the two. "I'm Gwendolyn Parrot." She extended her hand as if she were drawing a sword.

"I'm Ellen. Ellen Dodge." I shook her hand and tried not to wince at the iron grip. "This is my sister, Mimi."

Mrs. Parrot studied us through the thick lenses of her glasses. "We're delighted to have the two of you as part of our tour."

"We?" Mimi asked.

"Mr. Braddock is the tour leader, of course, whilst I am the Jane Austen expert. I'll be traveling with you to deliver the odd lecture, answer questions informally, that sort of thing."

Mrs. Parrot was no doubt nothing more than a sensible British matron, but for some reason, she made me uncomfortable. "Are you a professor at one of the universities?" I asked.

"Retired, dear. Tom asked if I would lend my expertise for the week, and I agreed."

Her answer was ordinary enough, but something about Mrs. Parrot didn't quite ring true. My mother had always had that typical British reserve, and Mrs. Parrot should have displayed the same thing, not such an obvious enthusiasm for meeting us.

"We're looking forward to learning more about Jane Austen," I said and tried to move past her, but she blocked my way again.

"Are you lifelong Austen devotees?" She was only making casual conversation. Given the chance to talk about their life's obsession, most people could chatter away forever. But something about this woman's eyes, the way she seemed to be sizing me up, made me uneasy.

"Our mother was the true Austen fan," I said. "I'm not sure either of us quite lived up to her hopes on that front."

She frowned. "*Hmm.* I see."

I see? What did that mean?

"Our mother was British," Mimi offered, but she wasn't looking at Mrs. Parrot. Instead, she cast her gaze over the woman's shoulder as she searched the room for the elusive Ethan.

"Your mother couldn't join you on the tour?"

I winced. Mrs. Parrot's question was innocent enough, but any reminders about my mother's death still stung.

"She passed away six months ago," I said.

"My condolences." Mrs. Parrot leaned forward and placed a hand on my forearm. "If there's anything I can do, please let me know."

What a strange thing to say. I looked more closely at her. She had to be seventy, at least, and tall enough to be imposing. I couldn't envision her tramping through Hampshire. Perhaps she would only be around in the evenings or when we stopped for lunch. I hoped that would be the case. I had enough to juggle without adding a nosy Austen expert to the mix.

"Thank you. But we're fine."

"Well, one never knows when something . . . unexpected might turn up. I mean . . . happen."

The champagne flute slipped from my fingers.

"Ellen!" Mimi shrieked and jumped away from the spray of liquid. Fortunately we were standing on a thick carpet, so the glass merely bounced instead of shattering.

"I'm so sorry." I looked down in dismay.

Mrs. Parrot wiped at the champagne droplets on her sensible tweed skirt. Not that you could actually see them against the mottled fabric. "It's no matter, dear. Entirely an accident, of course."

She straightened, and this time when our gazes locked, I was prepared. An electric jolt shot down my spine.

She knew about the diary.

"Ellen? Are you okay?"

I turned on my heel, and there was Daniel, looking concerned.

"Yes, yes. I'm fine. Just clumsy."

Mrs. Parrot looked seriously displeased at the interruption.

"Daniel!" Mimi threw her arms around his neck and hugged him. He flushed and looked uncomfortable, but then gently returned her hug.

"Hello, Meems. How are you?"

I'd forgotten how easily he'd picked up on my nickname for my sister. Just as I'd forgotten how he'd had her pegged from the moment he met her.

"A sweet kid," he'd said. "But a little . . . enthusiastic, isn't she?" He hadn't meant it in an unkind way, and though I probably should have been ashamed, his assessment of her had validated my own quiet reserve.

"What are you doing here?" Mimi finally released him. "It's been forever."

"Yes, it has." He looked at me, and then at Mrs. Parrot, and I realized he was waiting for an introduction.

"Mrs. Parrot? This is my friend Daniel Edwards. Daniel, this is Mrs. Parrot. She's the Austen expert on the tour."

"Glad to meet you," Daniel said. "Now, if you all don't mind, I'd like to steal Ellen for a minute—"

"Steal away!" Mimi practically shoved me into his arms. I caught my balance just in time.

I wasn't so easily disposed of though. "Will you be giving us an introduction to the tour this evening?" I asked Mrs. Parrot. It was the only way I could think of to avoid private conversation with Daniel. Even without factoring in the diary, the impact of seeing him again still had me reeling, and I wasn't ready for another tête-à-tête.

"I'll present a brief overview," Mrs. Parrot answered. "Some of the information may be repetitive for many of the participants, but I find it's best that we all start on the same page, as it were."

The same page of what? I still couldn't shake the feeling that Mrs. Parrot knew about the diary.

"I think it's time to take our seats for dinner," Daniel said. He put a hand lightly on the center of my back. "We're at this table over here."

His proprietary air, as courteous as it was, nettled me. I hadn't seen this man in more than fifteen years, and here he was acting as if it was only yesterday that he'd left me behind to live his own life.

I didn't want to make a scene though. I had to spend the next five days with all of these people, and true to my nature, I preferred to dodge the conflict rather than address it.

I allowed Daniel to steer me to the table, but when we got there, I turned to my sister. "Mimi? Why don't you sit here?" I pointed to the chair on my right. "And Mrs. Parrot? How about here?" I pulled back the chair to my left.

Mimi looked exasperated, as if I was clueless as to Daniel's intentions. "But—"

I pulled out my own chair and sat down. "This is wonderful, isn't it?" The forced note of cheer in my voice probably didn't fool anybody.

Mimi shot me a funny look, and Daniel shrugged. He took the chair on the other side of Mrs. Parrot. I shook out my napkin, placed it in my lap, and settled in for a very long evening of pretending.

somehow managed to make dinner conversation with Mimi and
Mrs. Parrot, with the occasional
comment to Daniel. After dessert,
Mrs. Parrot rose to her feet, and Tom tapped his spoon against
his glass. Everyone paused in their conversations. Since I was
sitting right next to Mrs. Parrot, I scooted my chair back so I
could see her. She cleared her throat, and I could only hope that
she hadn't been the long-winded kind of university professor.

"Tom has kindly asked me to give you a brief overview
of the tour," she said. "I know that some of you are here
for Jane Austen, while others are simply interested in walking the beautiful Hampshire countryside. This is the inaugural
Jane Austen tour for the company, so we want it to be a great
success."

There was a general murmur of assent and some head
nodding. I looked at Mimi, thinking we might exchange a

conspiratorial glance, but she was whispering something to Ethan, who had claimed the seat on the other side of her.

"We believe we can accommodate everyone's needs, whatever your preference might be." Mrs. Parrot nodded to Tom. "I will walk with you as I am able as well as driving the van, but I shall always be available for questions at breakfast and in the evenings."

Great. I had hoped to avoid her, but that clearly wasn't going to be possible.

"Tomorrow, we will make our way to Steventon, Jane Austen's birthplace. We'll also have a chance to visit the Vyne, a nearby country estate where the Austens occasionally dined, as well as the village church of Sherborne St. John, where Jane's oldest brother, James, was once the vicar."

I wondered if any of these places might have been my mother's choice for a final resting place, or if they held any clues as to what I was supposed to do with the diary.

"On Tuesday, we begin our walk in the lovely village of Upper Farringdon. We will walk to Chawton, where we will visit Jane Austen's House Museum as well as Chawton Great House, the country estate of Jane Austen's brother Edward Knight."

I had heard of all these places, of course, from my mother. I'd even seen pictures. And though I wasn't a devoted follower of Jane Austen, I was curious to see them.

"On Wednesday, we visit Chawton Woods, where Jane and her sister, Cassandra, often walked. We then take a train ride aboard the Watercress Line. Following that, we'll walk through Tichborne Park to our pub lunch. The afternoon will include a stroll along the river."

Mimi leaned over to me. "I feel tired already."

"Shh." I waved her away.

"On Thursday we travel to the beautiful village of Selborne. We'll walk extensively in the morning and then visit the home of Gilbert White, a renowned naturalist who was a contemporary of Jane Austen's father. We'll walk White's famous zigzag trail in the afternoon. And finally, on Friday we'll spend the morning in Winchester, where we'll see the house where Jane Austen was living at the time of her death. We will conclude our tour in a most fitting way, with a visit to Winchester Cathedral, where Jane Austen is interred."

"I hope everyone brought comfortable hiking boots," Tom joked, and the group joined in his laughter.

The dinner ended with a few people lingering over their coffee. Mrs. Parrot excused herself, which meant I had no buffer between me and Daniel. I kept trying to get Mimi's attention, but she was too engrossed in flirting with the newfound Ethan.

Daniel slid into Mrs. Parrot's vacant chair. "Ell, about the diary . . . " He paused. "Look, I know you've been through a lot. I don't want to be a bother. But we are friends, or we used to be. If I can help . . . " He had been leaning toward me as he spoke, but he realized what he was doing and straightened in his chair. "I just want you to know that I'm here for you."

"Thanks." I touched his arm lightly. "I appreciate that." The whole situation, though, was still so surreal. I couldn't allow myself to interpret Daniel's support as anything other than friendship. Not even if his mere presence made me feel far more alive than I had in years.

"Tell me about your business," I said. Changing the subject seemed the best means of self-preservation. "I don't remember you being interested in antiques in college."

He looked away for a moment and then back at me. "The antiques business belonged to Melissa's father originally. I've developed a specialization in tracking down rare objects. At least, that's my focus now. I've spent most of my career running the business from Chicago, but now I can do the part I really love."

"What kind of rare objects do you look for, when you're not helping out old friends?"

He froze for a brief second, and then relaxed again. If I hadn't known him so well, I would have missed his reaction. "Family heirlooms that have gotten away. Missing portraits. Keepsakes. That sort of thing."

Now I was the one who froze. Surely I was being paranoid, but . . . I mean, he was here to help me, right? That's why my mother had paid him.

"Do you deal in rare books?" I shouldn't have asked the question so pointedly, as if it were an accusation. Subtlety wasn't my forte under pressure.

He shrugged. "Occasionally, although my expertise is limited. I know enough to help you and Mimi."

Enough to help me and Mimi? Or enough to help himself?

I must have flinched at the thought, because Daniel's eyes darkened. "Ellen, I *will* help you and Mimi—"

I glanced at my watch. "It's late. I think I'm going to head back to my room." I stood up, and Daniel did the same.

"I'll walk you back," he said.

"No, thanks. Mimi's coming with me." I reached over and grabbed her arm, interrupting her flirtation with the London guy.

"What?" She looked at me, startled.

"Will you come back to my room with me? I need to talk to you. Estate business." I know that was the one thing that might pry her from the side of her London hottie.

Mimi looked as though she might balk, but Ethan smiled and rose to his feet. "I was just heading that way myself. I'll walk with you."

And that's how the four of us wound up crunching our way back across the path to the stable block. I hustled Mimi toward my door as quickly as I could, and with a few murmured goodnights to the men, I opened the door and shoved her in ahead of me.

⚜⚜⚜⚜⚜

"I'm really tired, Ell. This had better be good." Mimi flopped across my bed in her fancy dress. Normally she would have been worried about crushing the skirt, but intoxicated by her new romantic prospect, she didn't seem too concerned.

"'Good' may be in the eye of the beholder on this one." I wasn't sure how best to present the diary so that my sister would take it seriously.

Mimi plucked at the bedcovering. "I know we're supposed to work some sisterly bonding miracle while we're here, but"— she shot me a dubious glance—"it's a little late, don't you think?"

I froze. Why did I even bother trying to engage her? "We have a job to do this week," I said. "We don't have to like it, but if we want Mom's estate to be settled, we have to do it. For better or worse, we're stuck together for the next few days. We might as well make it bearable." I paused. "It might be the last time we see each other for quite a while."

Mimi didn't say anything, just picked at the duvet cover some more.

"I received something else from Mom's attorney before I left home."

Mimi grimaced. "What do we have to do now? Memorize *Sense and Sensibility* and recite it while standing on Jane Austen's grave?"

I was tempted to tell her yes, that's exactly what she had to do, but I didn't think I could keep a straight face.

"It's not another assignment. Well, not specifically, although I guess we'll have to come to some agreement about it."

I reached into the nightstand drawer and pulled out the diary.

"It's a book," Mimi said in a flat voice. "What's the big deal about a book?"

"Look at it." I pushed it into her hands. "Then you tell me what the big deal is."

I sat on the end of the bed and waited. I watched her face as she opened the cover, read the flyleaf, and then looked up at me with a bewildered expression.

"Remind me who Cassandra Austen is?" Mimi said. She'd never paid much attention to any of our mother's talk about her favorite author.

"Jane's older sister. Apparently they were always very close."

"Is this real?" Mimi looked incredulous.

I ran my hand over the duvet. "I think it's entirely possible that Mom made this thing up. Or had it made up."

"Then you don't think it's real?" Mimi began leafing through the pages. "It's a lot of trouble to go to for a hoax." She was quiet for a long time as she flipped from the beginning through to the end, not really stopping to read any of the entries. "How much would it be worth, if it's authentic?"

"If it were real, it would belong in a museum." I could already see the dollar signs in her eyes. "The instructions from the lawyer said we were to decide what to do with it."

Mimi looked at me with wide eyes. "It was Mom's. We're her heirs. Ergo, it's ours."

"Ergo?"

"We could ask that Parrot woman." Mimi looked up at me. "She could tell us what it's worth."

"No," I snapped.

She flinched at my vehemence. "What have you got against that old lady?"

"I think she already knows about the diary."

"How could she?"

"I don't know." I really didn't want to give too much credence to what was, at bottom, simply a bad feeling. I also didn't want to give Mimi any reason to go running to Mrs. Parrot.

"Did she say something to you?" Mimi asked.

"No. Not exactly."

"What then?"

"It was the look she gave me."

"The look she gave you." Mimi's voice dripped with disbelief.

"I could just tell that she knew."

She flopped on her back. "Give me a break. You're the sensible one, Ell. You don't go in for the woo-woo, intuitive stuff. That's more my style."

I wanted to protest at being so categorically dismissed, but she wasn't wrong.

"So what if Mrs. Parrot does know about the diary?" Mimi said. "It doesn't belong to her. It belongs to us." She was clearly not going to be swayed. "Have you read it?"

I shook my head. "I haven't had time."

"And Mom didn't send you any instructions with it?"

"No. Just the diary."

She laid it on the bed. "So what are we going to do now?"

"We don't tell anyone about it. Not yet." I gave my sister a stern look. "Agreed?" I wasn't going to tell her about Daniel. Not just yet. Let her think his presence was due to coincidence or even a long-lost romantic impulse. If she thought he could sell the diary tomorrow, she'd be driving him to an auction house so fast his head would swim.

"I still think we should ask Mrs. Parrot if it's real," she said. Her mouth had a mulish set to it. "What's she going to do, steal it from us?"

I grabbed the bed pillow and clutched it against my stomach. "Until we figure this out, we should keep it to ourselves."

"Where will we hide it then?" she asked.

"Here."

Mimi surveyed the interior of my hotel room. "Is there a safe?"

"No, but I'll find someplace."

"We should put it in a lockbox at reception."

"No. The fewer people who know about it, the better. We need to find out if it's real, and then decide who could best take care of it."

"Apparently not the owner," Mimi said, "since she's been dead since the nineteenth century."

"Look, Mom's instructions were for us to decide what to do with it. If we're going to make a decision, there's only one way to do that." I scooted to the head of the bed, shoved the pillow behind my head, and patted the mattress next to me.

Mimi groaned. "Not tonight, Ell. I'm exhausted. And we've got be up early."

"C'mon, Meems. Just a few pages." I wasn't above wheedling.

"All right. But just a few."

"I won't keep you up late."

"Well, if I don't get enough sleep, I'll look so haggard that yummy Ethan will never fall in love with me."

I rolled my eyes.

"What? It could happen." She nudged me. "All right, already. Let's read."

And that was how I found myself sitting next to Mimi while she took the diary and flipped open the cover.

"That Means You, Jane," she read out loud from the title page. "Sounds like sisters to me."

"Sounds like us," I added. "Let's just get on with it."

Mimi turned the first page and began to read.

10 January 1792

Jane disappeared again after our quarrel, and as there is no sign of Jack either, I can only assume they have escaped my mother's plans for their edification through diligent labour in the garden. I have warned Jane to guard her affections, for though he is a pleasant enough young man, he has no fortune and no connections. She is so young. Wherever she fancies, she pursues. I can only fear that the censure of our neighbors may turn upon her one day, if she cannot learn to conceal her feelings. She, of course, believes me to be a busybody, intent upon managing her affairs.

"I'm impressed you can even read her handwriting, it's so faded," I said. "I can't make heads or tails of it. Keep going." I nudged her.

Tom Fowle visited with us after Christmas, and though he has made no open declaration, I live in expectation. Jane chides me that he makes a poor romantic hero, but I am happy to wait and hope for the role of companion to a modest country vicar. The living he holds does not allow him to contemplate marriage at present. He said so to my mother at dinner when she quizzed him on his prospects and when he might return. He has hopes, though, of Lord Craven and the possibility of a second living to give him the means for an independent life and family . . .

The entry continued in the same vein—a mixture of Cassandra's clear affection for Tom Fowle, and her worry over Jane's relationship with the charming Jack.

Mimi read the last few lines of the entry, and when she finished, she closed the diary.

"Sounds like normal sister stuff to me," she said and then yawned so wide I thought her jaw might crack. "Some things never change, huh?"

"What do you mean?" I sounded defensive. Probably because I was.

"Older sisters always think they know what's best," Mimi said.

"And younger sisters are always rebelling," I added with a laugh. "You would think in a couple of centuries women would have learned something."

"Or they learned that some things never change."

Now that we'd read some of the diary, I felt strangely protective of Cassandra Austen, even if what we'd just read wasn't real. "Jane and Cassandra never married. They needed each other despite their differences."

Mimi frowned. "That's our problem, though, isn't it? We don't need each other."

She'd said it out loud, what the two of us had always known but tried to pretend wasn't true.

"It's not the same," I said, unwilling to meet her gaze. "Those were different times. Women were dependent on their families for support. They had to stick together."

"I don't think that matters." Mimi's voice was soft. "It's not a political statement, Ell. It's just the truth." She laid the diary on the bed. "We don't need each other. We haven't for a long time. And this trip isn't going to change that."

"Look, I'm sorry I said anything." The last thing I'd meant to do was to give Mimi the opportunity to play out another family drama. "It's late. We're tired. This diary has just complicated an already complex situation." I sighed. "I think we should get some sleep. We have a lot of walking to do tomorrow."

Mimi slid from the bed. "All right. We're not going to figure anything out tonight anyway."

It wasn't how I'd thought the evening would end, but it wasn't unexpected either. Mimi's feelings were hurt, she felt judged, and I was once again cast in the role of the bad guy.

Mimi paused at the door. "That diary is only one side of the story, you know. Too bad Jane didn't write down her own version."

"If she had, that would be a truly priceless book."

"A shame that wasn't what Mom sent us."

I laughed. "Go on. Get some sleep."

"Sure. You too."

I followed her to the door. After it shut, I leaned against it and contemplated the empty room.

Maybe if Mimi and I had been born two centuries earlier, we would have been compelled to get along better out of necessity. Maybe the modern world wasn't an improvement in some respects, at least not when it came to sisters.

I glanced through the bathroom door to my right at the gargantuan bathtub. In other ways, of course, the present was a far better deal. I decided to put the rubber duck to good use and fill the tub as full as possible with hot water and bubbles.

On the subject of bubble baths, I was sure, any two sisters could agree.

imi would never ap-
prove of my hiking shorts.
The elastic in the waist-
band would send her into
spasms, and the gray nylon fabric might really push her over
the edge. I untucked my plain white polo shirt. That at least
hid my stomach. Gray hiking boots and an olive green rain
jacket, which I cinched around my waist, completed my fashion
statement.

"I'm really not up for this," I said to my reflection in the
bathroom mirror. "Can't I call in sick?"

I wasn't sure where to stash the diary. I scanned the room,
deciding against a drawer in the nightstand or the dresser. If I
left it under the mattress, the maid might find it. In one corner,
a small bookshelf boasted a row of antique-looking books amid
the knickknacks. The books were clearly for ornamental purposes, not actual reading, and I doubted anyone ever paid much

attention to them, except when the maid flicked a feather duster over their tops.

"Perfect." I slid the diary into the row of books, not in the center but not on the end either.

The safety of the diary was ensured by its anonymity. I gathered up my daypack and my water bottle, slipped my room key in my pocket, and left to join the others.

They were waiting for me on the rear terrace. If Tom was irritated, he didn't show it. Mimi was happily ensconced at one of the tables next to her latest target. Daniel rose from his chair and came toward me.

"I thought we might be hiking buddies today."

"Great." I smiled the same forced smile I'd been using all my life.

Tom stepped into the middle of the group and motioned for us to gather around him. "Good morning, everyone. Today we'll set off for Steventon to see the site of the rectory where Jane Austen was born and where she spent the first twenty-five years of her life. For those of you who've never hiked before, let me give you a few tips."

I tried to ignore Daniel's presence next to me and concentrate on what Tom was saying, but how could I? Even after all these years, I could stand next to him and feel that strange, almost electric hum run through me.

"Please make sure to drink plenty of water. Also, let me know at the first sign of any problem with your boots. It's always best to stay ahead of blisters rather than treat them after the fact."

I looked over at Mimi. She and Ethan were whispering to one another and paying no attention to Tom at all.

"You'll soon find your natural pace. It's not necessary for everyone to stay together all the time. We'll stop periodically for everyone to catch up." Tom picked up his small backpack. "If there aren't any questions, then let's set off."

We made our way from the rear of the hotel, down the paved path I'd followed the day before, when I met Daniel. We moved onto a rutted footpath and began making our way around a field of grain that was knee high and a warm blue-green color, like the sea. England was exactly what I'd always pictured. Country lanes trimmed in green hedgerows, elegant stands of trees, a cloudless sky as blue as a robin's egg. If it hadn't been for the man next to me, I would have reveled in the beauty around me.

"I'm glad to see you again," Daniel said as we walked side by side where the path had widened to a dusty road. "I'm even happier you're still speaking to me. I didn't do a very good job of staying in touch."

I turned to him, surprised. "Why wouldn't I speak to you?" I forced my voice to its normal tone, but a spasm of panic tightened my belly.

"Ellen—"

"You don't owe me any apologies or explanations. I didn't keep up with many of my college friends. Most people don't."

"At the time, I didn't know that you—"

"The others are stopping up there. Maybe we should catch up." I wasn't about to let him open that can of worms. I'd never acknowledged my feelings to him when we were younger, and I certainly wasn't about to do so now.

I hurried forward to join up with Carol and Ralph, the couple from Nashville. I launched into some inane conversation and concentrated on keeping my boots moving, one in front of the other. We crossed beneath a railway line, and the tunnel offered some welcome shade. After skirting another field on another rutted path, we came to a field that was chest high in some kind of plant.

"Beans," Tom said with a sigh. "Somewhere in here there's a footpath, but we'll have to find it." Eventually he did locate the footpath, but it meant wading through a field of tall, scratchy beanstalks.

"I hope this is worth it," I said to Carol over my shoulder.

She laughed. "Don't trip, or we'll never find you."

We emerged from the field into a farmyard and then walked along a paved road for a bit. Tom came to an abrupt halt at a Y in the road.

"Where are we?" I asked. Daniel appeared at my side.

"Steventon, I think," he said. He was looking at me with a hint of sadness in his eyes that I decided to ignore.

"Where's the rectory?" I asked.

"If you'll gather over here," Tom was saying, "I'll give you a brief introduction."

The peace of the lush green meadow, the sheltering trees, and the quiet breath of the breeze stole over me as I waited for everyone to gather around Tom. This was where Jane Austen had been born and raised. No more than a wide spot in the road, it put the *b* in bucolic.

For the first time in months, I felt my jaw unclench and my muscles loosen, just a touch. I tried to set aside the turmoil of travel, my sister, Daniel—all the things that kept me anxious, even though I never showed it to the world. For a moment I just wanted to enjoy the serenity of the place.

"Welcome to Steventon," Tom said with a soft grin. "Not a lot of buildings to look at here, but the village—or what there is of it—lies just up the road." He pointed off at a right angle. "Where we're standing now is the site of the rectory from Jane Austen's day." Through a break in the hedge, he indicated the open field with its lone tree.

"Unfortunately, Austen's childhood home was built in a rather low spot. As a result, it was always damp. After her father's retirement, the family moved to Bath. Later, the house where she grew up was torn down, and a new rectory was built up there." He waved toward the rise on the opposite side of the road. "As you might guess, that house didn't have the same kind of problems with flooding and dampness, but eventually it was pulled down as well."

The group looked up toward the crest of the hill, and everyone chuckled. Tom continued for a few minutes, talking about

Austen's parents, her siblings, and life in a country parsonage at the end of the eighteenth century.

"Now we're going to walk up the lane here," Tom said, "to a spot with an actual building, and we'll see the church where Austen's father was the rector, and where she worshipped."

The group moved off down the lane, and I tried to lag behind, hoping that Daniel would go on without me. My hope was in vain. He quickly fell into step beside me. I could see Mimi twenty feet ahead, still tête-à-tête with Ethan.

"You haven't come to any of the class reunions," Daniel said as we walked along. I tried to focus on the sheer greenness of the scenery on either side of me, but I couldn't ignore him altogether.

"No. I couldn't get away."

"Work?"

"Something like that." But it hadn't been anything like that at all. The most recent reunion had happened last fall, when I took unpaid family medical leave so that I could drive my mother to radiation and chemo, make endless trips to the pharmacy for her medications, and hold her shoulders while she hunched over the toilet, alternating between sobbing and vomiting. Mimi had spent those months flying to New York. LA. Even Paris once.

"We missed you," Daniel said. "I thought we'd have a chance to catch up."

"I'm sorry about the divorce." Not the kind of thing you'd put in the alumni magazine, not that I still read it. "That must have been difficult."

He looked down at his feet. "Losing your mom must have been hard too."

"I had time to say good-bye."

"There's a lot to be said for that." He grimaced and then looked up at me, and for the first time since I'd encountered him on the path outside Oakley Hall, I thought I saw the real Daniel, the young man I remembered.

"Change hurts, whether it comes on gradually or happens in a split second." Daniel paused, and he seemed to take a deep breath. Then he swallowed what was obviously a lump in his throat.

"It's like the choice between ripping off the Band-Aid fast or peeling it off slowly. It hurts either way," I said. His divorce must have really taken a toll.

He turned his face to me, and our gazes met, locked in a moment of understanding. If we hadn't been walking down that lane at such a good clip, my knees might have buckled. That was the kind of moment that had made me love Daniel all those years ago. But I was older now. Much wiser. And much more protective of my heart.

"It was a hell of a Band-Aid," he said.

"I'm sorry. I didn't mean to trivialize—"

He looked away. "You didn't. Of course you didn't."

I shut my mouth then, determined to keep my foot out of it, but Daniel wasn't willing to walk in silence.

"Your mother, was she from Hampshire?"

"No. London. She was just utterly devoted to Jane Austen."

"But you're not?"

"I like her fine. But that kind of devotion to romance? It must skip a generation."

He laughed.

"What about your kids?" I asked. "Are your daughters following in their mother's Austen-loving footsteps?"

He shrugged. "They're more interested in whoever's on the cover of the teen magazines. Or those vampire books."

"How old are they?"

"Anna's nine, but Claudia's twelve going on twenty-five."

"Do you see them often?"

He gave me a funny look. "Of course."

"I'm sorry. I didn't mean to be nosy." I needed to change the subject. "Look. I can see the church." I'd let the conversation grow far more personal than I'd intended. "It's like something out of a book, isn't it?" I sped up my pace and moved away from Daniel before he could pick up on my distress. Daniel didn't make any attempt to keep up with me, and I refused to look back. Well, I refused to look back down the lane. If only I could have kept from looking back into my past.

I rounded the last bend in the lane, and there was the church, as idyllic and romantic as anyone could wish.

St. Nicholas, Steventon, had stood since Norman times and so boasted a square tower that had been topped by a Victorian steeple long after Jane Austen's day. It was sheltered on one side by a large yew tree, and the churchyard was dotted with weathered gravestones. Tom had mentioned that Jane's oldest brother, James, was buried there. He had been the rector after his father, after leaving Sherborne St. John.

As I moved closer to the church, though, I saw that Tom had drawn everyone aside into a gravel parking lot across the road. I paused for a moment, unsure what was happening, and then I spotted a large black hearse parked in front of the church, and my stomach sank.

The funeral procession emerged. A black coffin, covered with an enormous spray of bright flowers, was carried to the waiting vehicle. I was embarrassed at intruding on such a private moment, and I scurried into the car park across the road. Mrs. Parrot had pulled up the van there behind a screen of trees.

"We'll wait a bit and see if we can go inside once the service is finished," Tom advised us in a quiet voice.

I stood a little apart from the others, watching the current rector standing beside the hearse as the coffin was loaded inside. It was strange to be there as an observer, when not so long ago I'd been in the role of chief mourner. The knot in my stomach reminded me that my grief was still fresh. I glanced over at my sister, who was talking with Ethan. Mimi smiled as if she hadn't a care in the world, and the old resentment bubbled to the surface once more. How could she be enjoying herself? Didn't the sight of a funeral procession bother her at all?

The truth was that I had never understood my sister, just as she had never understood me. A hiking tour wasn't going to change that. Neither would a mysterious diary. If our mother's death couldn't bring us together, nothing could.

Mrs. Parrot was pouring water and handing around the cups. I took the one she offered me and gripped the plastic cup. I'd always known I was on my own in all the ways that mattered. It was time to quit hoping that things would change, no matter what side of the Atlantic I was on.

CHAPTER
SIX

than's longer legs made it difficult for me to keep up with him, but I had matched his stride all the way down the lane. Daniel had edged Ellen out of the herd, so to speak, and I silently cheered him on. He appeared to be as determined as I was in pursuit of his prey.

"So, will your office fall apart without you this week?" I asked Ethan as we stood in a parking lot across the road from the church. Tom had herded us there, where Mrs. Parrot was waiting with the tour van. She'd opened the rear door to reveal a morning snack and a selection of drinks.

"It always falls apart without me." He winked, which made my heart flip in my chest. I loved that feeling. I always had. "What about you?"

"I think the fashion industry will survive." Drat. I was hoping he'd give me some indication what he did for a living.

"I never asked you why you're here," he said. "Have you always been a fan of Jane Austen?"

I shook my head. "No. My mother's the true believer." I used the present tense without even thinking about it.

"Your mother, she didn't come with you?"

Too late I realized my mistake. Now I would have to take the conversation in a morbid direction, a situation I'd learned long ago to avoid with a new man.

"Actually, my sister and I are doing this walk more as a tribute to her." I lowered my voice to make it sound softer, more feminine. "We lost her six months ago." I paused a moment, which I thought was purely for effect, but sudden tears stung my eyes. "It seemed like the best way to honor her."

I should have been ashamed of myself, and part of me was. Ellen would have wrung my neck if she'd heard me, and my mother would have sighed in that deeply disappointed way she had. But she would also have been sympathetic in a way that Ellen never would. Mom understood the importance of getting and keeping a man. She'd learned the hard way what it meant to love and lose one, and the price had been high, both emotionally and financially.

I waited for Ethan to offer some more personal information, but he just gazed across the way at the church, where they were having some kind of service.

Unfortunately, I was starting to feel the effects of brand new hiking boots. I should have worn thicker socks, probably, but there'd been no time to pick them up at the outdoor store.

"Have you been on one of these walking tours before?" I asked him, trying to bring his attention back to me.

He turned away from the scene at the church. "No. But as I said last night, it seemed a good way to connect with my heritage."

"Is it what you were expecting?"

He looked down at me and smiled. "Not precisely. But it's beginning to have its compensations."

As flirting went, it wasn't the smoothest line ever, but at least he was making an effort. I had begun to worry that he wasn't interested at all.

I was about to try to find out about his job again when Tom joined us. "You two getting along okay?"

"Fine. Just fine." What I really wanted to say was "Go away," but I stopped myself just in time.

"No problems with any of your gear?" Tom eyed my brand new hiking boots with concern.

"We're fine. Thanks." Ethan didn't look very pleased with Tom's question.

"Everything's great." I winced at the banality of my response and at my overeager tone. I tried not to sound desperate, but I was bordering on it with Ethan. Why? Yes, I was getting older, but I didn't need to panic quite yet. Maybe it was because he was English. Or maybe it was everything that had happened in the past six months.

Tom moved away to speak to someone else, and we waited by the tour van. For some reason, Ethan now seemed distracted.

When the funeral procession finally departed and we made our way to the church, I noticed that he hung back.

"Aren't you going in?" I asked.

He shrugged. "I think churches all pretty much look the same. I prefer the graveyard anyway. More interesting."

I would rather have stayed with Ethan, but my blisters were burning, and I desperately needed to sit down for a few moments.

I followed the others up the path, through the doorway of the stone church, and into the cool, dim interior.

For me, going to church had always been like a fashion show, with pews on either side of the runway. So walking into Jane Austen's church was kind of a letdown, because I was wearing a moisture-wicking T-shirt, hiking capris that would have given Anna Wintour a stroke, and my cursed new hiking boots.

The blisters were stinging, but I was too proud to take my boots off and inspect the damage. The other people in the group dispersed around the little church to ooh and aah over the various pieces of Jane Austen memorabilia. I sank down on a pew halfway up the aisle and tried to forget about the flames of pain driving into the backs of my heels.

Of course I should have broken in my boots, but I couldn't find the time. Just like I couldn't find the time to get back to Dallas when Mom was sick.

Who was I kidding? Not myself. And certainly not God, especially in church. I hadn't taken the time to break in my boots because I simply hadn't wanted to. And I never made it back to see my mom in those last months because I had been afraid.

Ellen couldn't make me feel any guiltier than I already felt, although she was trying. She probably wasn't even aware of how she judged me. It was as ingrained a part of her nature as breathing. Just like being fun and flirtatious were ingrained in mine.

I sighed and pressed the small of my back against the pew in an attempt to ease my sore muscles. How did people ever manage to sit through an entire service on one of these torture devices?

"Mimi?" Tom appeared beside me. He'd been walking several members of the group around the church, pointing out various memorial plaques. I looked around. We were the only ones left inside.

"Is everyone waiting on me?" I started to stand up, but he waved me back to my seat.

"You're fine. Are you feeling okay?"

He knew about my blisters. I could tell. That both pleased and annoyed me. I liked being looked after. I always had. But to be honest, I would much rather he had been Ethan coming to check on me.

Tom sat down next to me. "What do you need? A plaster, as they say here? Amputation?"

"Better judgment would be nice." I wasn't normally the self-deprecating type, but despite Tom's military background and bearing, something about him encouraged me not to take myself too seriously.

"We put those warnings about breaking in your boots in the brochure for a reason." His words were stern, but his tone was light.

"I figured that out about a hundred yards in."

"In all seriousness, do you need some help?"

I had always found it so easy to play the damsel in distress. It generally worked like a charm. If Ethan had been sitting next to me, I would have milked it for all it was worth. Instead, I shook my head. "I have that blister stuff in my pack." Well, technically, Ellen had something in her pack, but we were sisters, so it was true for all intents and purposes.

"I don't want you to be miserable. Let me know if you can't walk. Mrs. Parrot is still here with the van."

"No. Then I'll be a marked woman for the rest of the tour."

"Better safe than—"

I didn't want him to keep harping on my lack of preparedness, so I decided to change the subject. "Why Jane Austen?"

He paused to indicate he'd gotten the message. Then his gaze shifted toward the front of the church. The white walls on each side of the interior looked as if they were coated with lime, but near the front it had been cleaned away to reveal some older detailing in tones of terra-cotta and gray.

"This tour was a special request, actually, but once I started to put it together, I knew I was on to something." His gaze slid around the church. "Can you think of any place more peaceful? Not a bad place to spend my days."

"You didn't want to go back to the States when you retired?"

He shrugged. "I spent most of my career overseas. Gayle and I never really put down roots anywhere. After she died . . . well, I learned that home is about the people, not the place."

"Do you have family anywhere?" Despite my personal rule of not engaging in conversation with men who were more interested in me than I was in them, I found I wanted to know more about him.

"I have a daughter who lives in Texas."

"What part?"

"Houston."

"I'm from Dallas." As soon as I said it, I realized how idiotic it sounded. I had to laugh. "People always say that, like 'Oh, Texas. Maybe I know them,' when there must be twenty million people in the state."

"About twenty-five, I think," Tom said with a smile. "But you never know."

"No, you never do." We shared a grin. How long had it been since I'd laughed at myself in front of a man, even one in whom I had no romantic interest? It felt liberating, and I hadn't even realized I'd been captive to anything.

"Do you see your daughter often?"

"As much as I can. She stays pretty busy with her own life."

He said the words in all innocence, but they hit home. Had my mother ever said the same thing to someone she'd just met? Had she worn that same sad expression, the one that mixed love, forgiveness, and pride?

"I'm sure she does the best she can."

Tom smiled, but there was that sadness again. "She does." He leaned back in the pew. "It's just the way things are."

I had a feeling it was more the way of inattentive daughters, but there was no need to point out to him what he no doubt already knew.

"So," he said, "are your feet rested enough to continue on? We have a good distance to go before lunch."

"Lead on, Major."

He rose to his feet with a grin. "Actually, it's Colonel. But I'd much rather you just called me Tom."

"Absolutely."

We walked out of the church together, and an older woman, probably a member of the church, stayed behind to lock up.

"See that tree?" Tom said, pointing to the enormous yew that stood next to the church. "That's where they used to keep the key."

"The key?"

"To the church." He nodded toward the door. "It looked like a skeleton key on steroids. A foot long or so." He indicated the approximate length with his hands. "In Jane Austen's day, the whole village knew it hung inside the trunk of the tree. When they needed to go inside, everyone knew where to find it."

"And now? Surely they don't still use it."

"No. Someone stole it recently. So they couldn't even use it if they wanted to."

I looked at him in surprise. "Who would steal the key to a church?"

"Austen collectors can be a funny bunch. They'll take anything that's not nailed down."

Like a diary? I hoped Ellen had found a good hiding place in her room. "So, what, there's like a black market in Jane Austen memorabilia?" I tried to keep my tone light, but his words sent my pulse skittering.

"Yes, believe it or not."

We had reached the road. The others were walking back in the direction we'd come. "Are they that valuable?" I asked. "Things that belonged to Jane Austen or have some connection to her?" My mouth went dry. Surely Tom couldn't know anything about the diary.

"Very valuable. First editions of her works can sell for thousands and thousands of pounds. Imagine what her personal possessions might bring."

I could imagine only too well. I could envision the auction hammer going down, and my future as a New York business owner taking off.

"Too bad about the key though." Cassandra's diary might have been a bit . . . contraband, but at least it didn't belong to God or anything like that.

"With any luck they'll find it someday," Tom said. "Come on. We'd better catch the others."

I followed him as best as I could, wincing as one of my blisters rubbed against my boot.

I was used to juggling a lot of things at once, but right now I had too many balls in the air. My mother's ashes to scatter. My relationship with my sister to sort out. Ethan. Tom's attentions. And that problematic diary, which might or might not be real, might or might not be worth a fortune, and might or might not allow me to live out my dreams.

Who would have thought that things could get so complicated in a sleepy little place like Hampshire?

 noticed that Ellen was walking by herself as we passed the few houses that made up the village of Steventon and cut through a pasture toward Deane, where Tom said we would eat lunch. Ethan had joined me once again, and we chatted while we walked along more fields and under a railway bridge, then a stand of trees. Trains to London sliced through the tranquil landscape every few minutes. Ethan said they were full of "ladies who lunch," headed to the city for the day.

I was getting a little more adept at climbing over turnstiles, those awkward wooden steps that allowed us to make our way over fences, but I had more trouble with the heat. Sweat poured off my forehead, and I was sure my curls were frizzing out of control. The fact that Ethan still wanted to walk beside me was a testimony to his interest in me . . . or at least I hoped that it was.

We skirted the park of a huge house that we could only glimpse through the foliage, and then made our way down the slope of a pasture to the scolding bleat of several sheep, who didn't seem too happy to share their turf.

A church spire rose out the trees, and I could see the edge of another house beyond.

"We're almost to Deane," Ethan said.

"You really do know this area." I was impressed.

He shrugged. "Actually, that would be my house, just there past the church."

"Is it one of those charming cottages?" Even though I had my sights set on New York City and urban life, I could appreciate the beauty of an English cottage.

"You'll see," Ethan answered with a grin and a wink.

We reached the fence at the bottom of the pasture and climbed over one last stile. The church to our left boasted a substantial square tower with four turrets on the top. A paved walk led past the church, and then I saw it.

Ethan's house.

Now to me a house was a three-bedroom ranch in a Dallas suburb. This wasn't a house. This was a mansion.

I think the house was Queen Anne style. All I knew was that I immediately fell in love with the length of its red-brick frame, the white trim of the multi-paned windows, the climbing vines and sheltering shrubberies, and the various chimneys that dotted the roof.

"This is your house." I meant to ask that as a question, but it came out a statement.

Ethan looked pleased at my astonishment. "Do you like it?"

"How could I not?" I turned to look at him. "Does Tom know that's your house?"

"I have no idea." He smiled at me. "Perhaps after dinner tonight, you'd like to come back for a tour?"

I paused. *Don't be overeager.* I bit my lip and tried to look indecisive, although my answer was never in doubt.

"Just for a quick look around," I said. "Maybe Ellen can come with us." I only said that because I knew she'd never agree to do it.

"Of course. If that's what you'd like." He didn't look very pleased about adding my sister to the guest list, which made me even happier.

Tom let the group linger for a few minutes to admire the house and take pictures. He explained that the Harwood family had lived in the house during Jane Austen's time, and that Jane no doubt would have visited.

I stood on the paved walk, a little apart from the group, and slowly turned in a circle as I thought about everything we'd seen that morning. It was only our first day, but something felt . . . different, I guess you'd say. It was a lot to take in, Jane Austen–wise, and for some reason, it felt as though my mother was there in a way. Probably because she always had been, in her heart.

"Lunch awaits," Ethan said. I hadn't noticed that he'd come to stand beside me. "The pub is just on the other side of the main road."

I had visions of a very cold drink and lots of air-conditioning. "Let's not dawdle then," I said with a laugh. I was hot, tired, and sweating, but for the first time in a while, and despite my blisters, I felt okay.

✣✣✣✣✣

Mimi was making a spectacle of herself with Ethan, but I didn't care. Really, I didn't. I just wanted to get out of the sun and sit quietly for a few minutes. Tom shepherded the group across the busy road. The pub was all dark beams and plaster, with a sloping roof and flowers blooming in every planter and basket.

The interior of the pub was quaint, with its dark paneling, carpets, and fireplace. It was also hot, more suited to a cold winter evening than a freakishly warm summer day. We made our way to the bar to secure drinks—ah, the glories of diet soda on tap—and then settled in at a table beneath the bay window. The pub dog, an aging yellow creature called Harry, made the rounds, eager for attention.

I sat near the open window, and Tom sat next to me. I saw his gaze travel to the other end of the table, where Mimi and Ethan were flirting.

"I'm worried about her feet," Tom said. It was probably the antithesis of whatever romantic sentiments Ethan was currently whispering in Mimi's ear.

"I warned her to break in those boots before she came."

Tom contemplated the contents of his glass on the table in front of him. "I offered to bandage her up, but she wouldn't let me help. You should keep an eye on her."

A smile played at the corners of my mouth, but I suppressed it. I had no doubt that Tom would keep enough of an eye on Mimi for the both of us.

"What should I tell her to do this evening?" I asked instead. "Should she soak her feet?"

"Treat the blisters with rubbing alcohol, if she can stand it. Just have her keep her feet as dry as possible. It's usually the combination of moisture and friction that causes the problem."

"Or the lack of foresight and planning," I said with a sigh. I kept hoping that someday Mimi would learn, but judging from the state of her feet and the way she was flirting with Ethan, it seemed that it was not going to be that day.

"Just keep an eye on her." Tom frowned at Ethan.

"Not just her blisters?" I prompted. I assumed that Tom's concern stemmed from worry about Mimi rather than anything specific he knew about Ethan.

He grimaced. "I hoped I wasn't that obvious."

I placed a hand on his where it rested on the tabletop. "Don't worry. Everyone else is so busy watching them flirt, they won't notice . . . anything else."

"Did you know Ethan before the tour?" I asked. "I understand he's local."

Tom shook his head. "Not personally. I only knew *of* him."

"*Of* him?"

Tom frowned and looked a bit furtive. "It's nothing."

"Tom—"

"Just tell your sister not to get her hopes up. Ethan has something of a . . . reputation already in Hampshire."

"And in London, too, no doubt," I murmured. Tom didn't disagree.

Our food arrived, and I decided to put my worries over my sister aside long enough to eat. I examined my ploughman's lunch with appreciation. The plate overflowed with big chunks of fresh-baked bread, a hearty slab of Sussex cheddar, celery and apples, and a pickled onion.

"I feel like I've earned this," I said to Tom with a grin.

"You have. We covered about six miles this morning."

"Six?" I didn't know whether to laugh or cry. "How many more do we have to go today?"

Now Tom laughed. "Not nearly that many."

We spent the rest of the meal in pleasant conversation. He was an intelligent, well-rounded man who could talk on almost any subject.

"Would it be rude to ask where you live?" I asked as we finished the meal.

"I'll tell you where I live if you tell me why Daniel Edwards looks like he wants to clean my clock."

I'd forgotten about Daniel, who was seated at the other end of the table next to Mimi.

"He's an old college friend, actually, but I haven't seen him in years."

Tom gave me a long look. "An odd coincidence, both of you turning up on this tour."

I reached for my glass and drained the remains of my diet soda. "Yes. Isn't it?"

"Are you stalking him or is he stalking you?" Tom asked with a twinkle in his eye.

"Neither. But I think we may both be the victims of some matchmaking from beyond the grave."

"Your mother?"

"The original believer in Austen's happy endings. Even though her own marriage was a disaster."

"Hope springs eternal, *hmm?*"

"Something like that."

"Seems like a nice guy," Tom said but his praise sounded a bit cautious.

"He is. But college was a long time ago. People change."

"Not always as much as you might think." Tom's glance flicked toward Ethan again, and that look made me wonder again what he knew that he wasn't telling me.

Tom looked at his watch. "I should round up the troops. Time to ship out, since the taxi's here." He nodded toward the door, and I could see a silver minivan next to the one belonging to the tour company. "We'll ride from here to the Vyne," he said.

Our conversation left me feeling unsettled. Mimi wouldn't like it, of course, my interfering in her budding romance, but I trusted Tom's judgment. When I saw her get up and walk toward the bathroom, I couldn't help but follow her.

Mimi turned when I entered the restroom. The tiny women's restroom held two sinks, two stalls, and a lot of humidity.

"Hey, sis." She was beaming from ear to ear.

How could I do it? How could I crush her hopes? The fit she'd pitched about the facial the day before told me she was feeling insecure about her looks, but I had to choose. Was it better for me to make her angry by warning her about Ethan, or was it better to let Ethan break her heart?

"Meems, maybe you should . . . I don't know. Slow it down a little bit."

Her shoulders went rigid. "Slow what down a bit?"

Of course she knew exactly what I meant, but it was part of the game we'd always played.

"With Ethan. I mean, we're here for a specific reason. I don't want us to lose focus. We should be thinking about where we want to . . . leave Mom."

Her eyes narrowed, which was never a good sign.

"Quit fretting," Mimi said. Her eyes flashed. "Go find Daniel, give him a kiss that will rock his world, and tell him you want to get married and have lots of babies." She laughed, but it wasn't a nice sound. "What could be simpler?"

"I'm not fretting," I snapped.

Mimi flushed. "Don't be so sensitive—"

I turned on my heel and left the bathroom.

"Ellen! Wait!"

I bolted through the main door. On the way in, I'd noticed a garden to the side of the pub. I slipped through the open gate, but Mimi followed me.

"Ellen, wait."

I stopped and slowly turned to face her.

"We have to talk," Mimi said. "Sit down for a minute." She stepped toward one of the wooden tables that dotted the garden. "I didn't mean to offend you."

I wanted to give my sister's trite apology the cold shoulder it deserved. But even more, I longed for some comfort, a little understanding, anything really that would assuage the hurt.

"Please, Ell. Let's talk."

This time, I heard real regret in her voice. "Okay," I said.

She led me to a table in the corner, and we sat down, but I couldn't bring myself to look her in the eye. Her dismissive attitude toward my pain still stung.

"What's going on?" Mimi laid her hands, palms down, on the dark, polished wood.

"It's not really about you," I said.

"Then tell me what it is about." She paused, and a look of horror crossed her face. "You're not sick, are you?"

I didn't answer immediately, and her hands trembled.

"Ellen? Are you sick?"

"No. No, of course not."

"Ellen, I'm sorry."

"You don't have to apologize."

She shook her head. "I don't mean about this." She sighed. "We probably needed this. No, I mean that I'm sorry I wasn't more help at the end, the last six months with Mom."

"You would have come if you could." I didn't actually believe that, but we'd had enough drama for one day. Time to be magnanimous.

"No, I wouldn't have. I mean . . . I didn't." She paused. "It's just that . . . I was afraid."

"So was I." I grimaced. "I didn't mean that to sound judgmental. I just meant—"

"Maybe we're more alike than we think," Mimi said.

"What do you mean?"

"You're afraid to show your feelings to the man you love, and I'm afraid of what will happen if I can't hide mine."

I ignored her reference to Daniel. "Mom would never have expected you to be unemotional."

"No, but you would have, Ell. If I'd shown up on the doorstep crying my heart out, you would have seen me as another burden to bear."

"I wouldn't have." But I knew Mimi was right. If she had come home during those months, I wouldn't have wanted her to be *her*. I would have wanted her to be like me.

"You're right," I finally said. "I'm sorry." And then it occurred to me that maybe I was just as much to blame for Mimi missing Mom's last few months as she was.

We were both quiet for a long moment.

"You really should give Daniel a chance," Mimi said, breaking the silence.

"A chance to do what?"

"C'mon, Ell. He's practically been glued to your side since the welcome dinner."

"Just because he's on his own, and I'm the only person he knows." Of course, she didn't know that Mom had basically hired him to be glued to my side, as she put it.

"Not true. He knows me."

"But you've been glued to Ethan, so you're not really an option. Daniel's just an old friend."

"I think he came on this trip because of you."

I laughed. "I appreciate your faith in my middle-aged charms."

"You're not middle-aged," Mimi said.

"You only say that because we're so close in age. You don't want to be implicated."

Mimi giggled, a soft, melodic sound that could charm even a cranky older sister.

We sat beside a large bed of roses, and their heady perfume filled the air. In an English garden, it was hard to believe that bad things existed in the world. That all the problems in my life existed. If only I could have stayed there forever.

But we couldn't, of course. At that moment, Tom appeared around the gate.

"There you are. We'd better get going."

We followed him to the parking lot and climbed into the waiting taxi, since the van was already full. As we pulled away from the pub, I wondered if the confrontation between Mimi and me would help or hurt our chances of agreeing on where to leave Mom, much less what we were going to do with Cassandra's diary.

At least we were speaking to each other honestly, if a little guardedly. That was some improvement.

CHAPTER
EIGHT

By the time we reached the Vyne, an enormous house that now belonged to the National Trust, I would have given my kingdom for a bucket of ice, and then I would have dumped it over my head. Even with the air-conditioning in the taxi, I was feeling the heat. Mimi, of course, looked as cool and beautiful as ever.

"Unfortunately, we only have a short time here," Tom informed us as we made our way up a gravel path toward the house. The trees and grass were still green but had wilted in the heat. I could identify with that.

"The Vyne was the home of the Chute family, and Jane Austen dined here on occasion. We know that her older brother James visited here on Sundays, as it was the Chutes who gave him the living of the parish at Sherborne St. John, where we're going next."

The car park where we'd left the van and the taxi were in the rear of the house, so we approached the Vyne through an enormous garden that bordered an ornamental lake. Swans glided on the murky surface. As we drew nearer to the house, we came upon more formal gardens with well-tended hedges and flowers. Finally, the walk led us to the rear of the house.

The back of the Vyne was even more imposing than the front of the home, which we'd seen from the road on our way in. It was almost as wide as the lake, with an enormous central pediment supported by huge columns. On each end, smaller wings protruded from the main body of the house.

"Unfortunately, Mrs. Chute didn't care for Jane Austen," Tom said as we gathered around him, "and so Jane's presence here was much more infrequent than her brother's."

He came to a stop on the walk in front of the pediment. "Those of you who want to see inside the house can take the whirlwind tour and then ride in the van with Mrs. Parrot to Sherborne St. John. For those who prefer to keep walking, we'll explore some of the woodland area of the park and then make our way to the village. Of course, anyone who would like to rest can remain with Mrs. Parrot while the others tour the house."

While everyone else dispersed, I hung back. Could I question Mrs. Parrot without arousing suspicion, especially when I already thought she knew more than she was saying?

Mrs. Parrot raised a hand to shade her eyes and surveyed the lawn and the lake. "There's a bench in the shade." She gave me a shrewd look. "Shall we?"

"Sounds good." I followed her, careful to avoid the duck droppings that littered the withered grass as we crossed the large lawn that separated the enormous house from the lake.

"Mind your step," Mrs. Parrot said over her shoulder, and I wondered if she was referring to the conversation we were about to have or the duck droppings.

I settled onto the bench. Though the temperature couldn't have been more than seventy-five degrees, it felt much hotter. A thin breeze wafted from the direction of the lake.

"Now then." Mrs. Parrot settled her shopping bag at her feet. "You have some questions, I think."

It was the understatement of the year, but I had to look like an ordinary Austen fan, nothing more. "I'm afraid I'm a little rusty on my facts when it comes to Jane Austen." I kept my tone casual.

"Most people are, dear." Her tone was condescending but not unkind. "How may I help?"

"I was wondering about her relationship with her sister. I mean, I know everyone says she and Cassandra were close."

"*Hmm.* Yes, they were, by all accounts."

"How do we know that?"

Mrs. Parrot looked off into the distance. "From Jane's surviving letters, for the most part. The bulk of them, at least the ones that remain, were written to her sister."

"The ones that remain?"

A strange expression crossed Mrs. Parrot's face, a look of both weariness and a certain furtiveness. "Jane instructed her sister to destroy most of her correspondence after her death."

"And she did?"

Again, Mrs. Parrot looked . . . odd. "That's the general belief."

"Didn't Jane and Cassandra ever disagree?" I asked, although I had evidence of the very fact in my possession. Cassandra had clearly not approved of Jane's affection for Jack Smith.

"I'm sure they must have done. But if they did, they kept it between themselves."

"So these letters don't give any hint of a conflict between them?"

"No. But then letters in their day would have been far more public. Their contents would have been read to the rest of the family around the fire in the evening."

"All of them?"

"Not all, of course. But for the most part, such communications would have been shared."

I let my gaze travel across the expanse of the lake. A few brave picnickers risked the sun and the duck droppings. If what Mrs. Parrot said was true, Cassandra Austen's diary, her authentic diary, would have information no one had ever known about the Austen sisters. It would indeed be a priceless treasure.

I hesitated over my next question, afraid to tip my hand, but in the end, I had to take the risk. "What about diaries? Is that where they would have kept their secrets?"

Mrs. Parrot didn't bat an eyelash at my question, but her feet shifted, brushing the shopping bag. "Ah, the holy grail of all things Austen."

"What do you mean?" I hoped my face concealed my emotions as well as Mrs. Parrot's did.

"No one has ever offered any proof of their existence," she said, "But it's also very unusual that they wouldn't have kept them."

"So there might be one somewhere?" It hadn't even occurred to me to wonder about Jane Austen's diary. I'd been so absorbed in Cassandra's.

Mrs. Parrot shook her head. "There's no reason to believe such diaries exist." She looked up at me, her gaze intense. "Although one never knows," she added.

I knew from my mother that, occasionally, Austen-related items turned up from time to time. Most of them—like Jane's famous writing desk—had been in the possession of her brothers' descendants before they were donated to museums and the like.

"So it's not beyond belief that her diary might turn up?" *Or Cassandra's*, I added to myself.

"Conceivable, yes. Likely, no."

I didn't believe Mrs. Parrot's nonchalance. It was too . . . studied, as Jane Austen herself would have said.

We sat in silence for several minutes as I turned this new information over in my mind. The diary my mother had given me might actually be real. And if it were . . .

"We should be going." Mrs. Parrot tapped the watch affixed to the lapel of her jacket. How she could stand to wear a tweed blazer in this heat, I had no idea. The English were made of sterner stuff than we wilting Americans.

"Okay." I followed her back across the lawn and gave a last, wistful glance toward the magnificent house. I wondered how Jane Austen might have felt when she visited. The numerous windows, the huge columns, the vast pediment, and the sheer size of the place must have dwarfed anything else she knew, even her father's church. The Vyne was a far cry from her father's humble rectory in the obscure village of Steventon. I felt overwhelmed just looking at it.

We met up with the rest of the group on the path back to the parking lot. Mimi limped along, a forced smile plastered on her face. She shot hopeful glances at Ethan, but he seemed intent on what one of the Austenites was telling him about the care and cultivation of rose gardens.

We paused near the entrance, and I ducked into the small refreshment stand, looking for a Diet Coke. My stealth was rewarded—but when I emerged, I stumbled across a conversation clearly not meant for my ears.

"She asked about diaries." Mrs. Parrot's voice came from behind the refreshment stand, but I couldn't hear the mumbled response, although the voice was clearly masculine.

Before I could walk around the corner to find out, Mimi appeared at my elbow. "Hey, sis. Where'd you get the Diet Coke?"

The other conversation stopped abruptly. It was too late to shush her.

"I got it in here." I strained to hear any more from behind the refreshment stand, but all was quiet. "Come on," I said to Mimi with a sigh. "I'll buy you one."

We went back into the refreshment stand, Mimi limping after me. As I forked over my pound coin and a fifty-pence piece, I could only wonder if anyone on this walking tour was who or what they appeared to be, and who else knew about Cassandra's diary.

CHAPTER NINE

ven my sister Ellen would agree that beauty worthy of Ethan took extra time, so I was a little late for dinner that night. Tom had told us that the dining room at Oakley Hall had once been a monument to Jane Austen, but as he explained before the meal was served, the management had recently redecorated. Gone were the portraits of the Austen family, various prints that depicted Jane's parents, sister, and brothers. The only existing portrait of Jane was a small watercolor sketch, currently housed in the National Portrait Gallery in London—a portrait that all of her family agreed looked nothing like her. So instead of eating dinner under the noses of the Austen family, we sat in modern chrome black-and-white splendor.

Ethan sat next to me. Even after abandoning me at the church at Steventon to wander in the churchyard, he couldn't have been more attentive. He collected art and antiques, owned a house nearby, was practically a descendant of Jane Austen, and made me forget the gnawing pain on my toes and heels. My skin still burned from where Ellen had doused my blisters with rubbing alcohol on the advice of Tom Braddock. Fortunately for him, Tom sat at the other end of the table.

"Is the lamb to your taste?" Ethan asked. He leaned toward me, grinning with a devilish air. "I don't suppose it can be as delicious as the company."

If an American had said that, I would have found it cheesy, but a posh British accent tends to make everything more attractive.

"It's lovely. And the monkfish?"

"Adequate." He winked, though, to take the sting out of his response. "But again, not nearly as tasty as—" He broke off and stared meaningfully at my lips.

I forced myself to stay seated, and not leap up from the table and do the happy dance around the dining room. The other members of the group were watching us. I could feel it. Some just darted glances, while others observed more openly. I didn't care. Why would I? Somewhere in the middle of a Hampshire wheat field, a miracle had happened. I had finally found the man of my dreams.

Now I just had to convince him that I was the woman of his.

I had been ignoring Ellen, who sat on the other side of me, but she seemed content to talk about all things Austen with the couple across the table. I'd long ago learned to tune out those conversations.

"I'm excited to see your house," I said to Ethan. "I'm sure it's as charming inside as it is outside."

"It's a bit of a mess at the moment, I'm afraid. But it does have the usual conveniences. As well as the requisite sheep." He was enjoying this very much, but I didn't care if he was laughing at me a little. That house must have had at least twenty rooms, not to mention a breathtaking vista overlooking a good deal of parkland.

"How many sheep does it take to meet the 'requisite' standard?" *Careful, Mimi. Keep it light. And don't let him hear the* ka-ching *of the cash register in your head.*

It wasn't that I was a gold digger. Most of the guys I'd dated over the years had made a good living, but none of them had been seriously wealthy. I was a modern woman, and while I liked a man to pull his own weight, I didn't expect him to pull mine. But even a modern woman didn't mind being spoiled from time to time.

"I think fifty meet the requirement. It would take that many again to achieve 'extraordinary.'"

Really, how could I not fall for this man? Handsome, charming, rich. With a nicely dry sense of humor. True, he didn't seem to be too handy when it came to the mundane aspects of life, like blisters, but given his other attributes, I thought he could be forgiven that minor failing.

"When should we leave?" I asked. "We may have to sneak away from Tom."

"Now? During dinner?" He laughed again.

"No, of course not. After dinner. Even a fabulous house isn't worth missing dessert."

The truth was, of course, that by that point, I couldn't have cared less about dessert. But I had gotten to this stage in a relationship often enough to know that I had to achieve a delicate balance between interest and eagerness. Not enough of the first, and he'd wander off looking for a more appreciative audience. Too much of the latter, and he wouldn't be wandering off; he'd be running for the door.

He looked at me with an impish light in his eyes. "As soon as you've eaten the last bite of dessert, we'll go."

Ellen would have my hide, of course. We were supposed to read some more in that might-be-real-but-probably-isn't diary before we went to sleep. Surely, though, she'd understand that spending the evening with the man of my dreams had to take priority. Even Jane Austen would have approved of that.

❧❧❧❧❧

Ethan's car was a low-slung, black BMW that raced along the two-lane road toward Deane with breathtaking speed. I forced my eyes to stay open so that I wouldn't look afraid. Riding on the wrong side of the road was nerve-racking enough. Doing it at a high rate of speed sent my pulse skittering.

Thankfully, the thrill ride didn't last long. What had taken a good part of the afternoon to cover on foot took only minutes in Ethan's car.

He turned into a side road by the pub where we'd had lunch and then into a driveway.

"How long ago did you inherit the house?" I asked.

"I just took possession last month," he said. "It may be in a state with workmen everywhere."

"At this hour of the night?" It was past ten o'clock.

He chuckled. "I doubt they're present at the moment, but they may have left everything a bit of a mess. The house was in a terrible condition."

I smiled to reassure him. "I'm used to . . . what did you call it? Chockablock?" I was glad to have a chance to return the teasing. It kept the balance of power a little more even.

He pulled up behind the house into a paved parking area. "Come on." He didn't come around to open my door, so I did it myself and followed him through a wisteria-framed gate in a brick wall.

Even in the last remnants of daylight, I could see what a wonderland the garden was. Jewel-toned flowers spilled from containers and beds. Ornamental trees, a scattering of benches, and a fountain in the middle completed the idyll.

"It's breathtaking," I said.

Ethan paused. "Yes. Yes, I suppose it is."

He took it for granted of course, this earthly paradise. If you were accustomed to this kind of grandeur, maybe it got tedious after a while. Maybe you flopped on one of those benches and yawned with boredom. All I wanted to do was slip off my sandals and perch on the edge of the fountain with my feet in the water. The scent of honeysuckle hung thick in the air.

"Let's go inside." He took my elbow and led me to a wooden door that must have once been a servants' entrance. We ducked inside, and I found myself in a kitchen straight out of my mother's favorite magazine, the *English Home*. Slate floor, a shiny new Aga cooker tucked into the enormous original fireplace, a battered farmhouse table, and a huge stone sink underneath the windows at the far end. It was a kitchen fit for Cinderella. Rustic and romantic at the same time.

"Do a lot of cooking, do you?" I said to Ethan with a sidelong look. "Or is this just to impress the women you bring here?"

"Definitely to impress the women." He turned toward me and took my hand. Then he pulled me closer and looped his arms around my back. "Is it working?"

I didn't dare tell him how well.

"I assume there's more to the house than the kitchen."

He chuckled. "Yes. If you insist, although I prefer the view here."

Oh, he was good, but I wasn't going to let him go too fast.

"Show me the rest."

He did, flipping on the lights as we went from room to room. He was right. The house did need some serious updating, not to mention a few minor repairs. The bathrooms were a bit of a mess, as he'd said, but the guest bedrooms retained their faded country-house chic, with lots of antique furniture, toile curtains, and chairs upholstered in fabric thick with cabbage roses.

"Did you inherit the house furnished?" I asked as we stood in one of the guest bedrooms, and I admired the four-poster bed and the jumble of collectibles on the mantelpiece—vases, figurines, even some wrought-iron pieces.

"Yes, it was fully furnished." He laid a hand on a large cabinet, almost as big as a wardrobe. He ran his hand down the side of it. "Late Georgian. An Austen family heirloom from her niece, Fanny."

"That's not a wardrobe?"

He shook his head. "Not exactly. And this"—he moved toward the small table that stood between two tall windows—"is a writing desk. See how this tilts?" He pulled the top toward him, and it lowered to form a flat surface. "Jane Austen could have written her novels on it."

"Or her diary." I paused. Ellen would kill me, but Ethan would be impressed. Besides, he might be able to help us with authenticating our supposed treasure.

"My mother left us an Austen heirloom. At least, we think it might be. We're not sure."

"Really?" He looked skeptical. "Something decorative, like a mirror or a soup tureen? I'm afraid there are a number of counterfeit—"

"It's Cassandra's diary, actually." I tried to sound casual. I turned away so that my expression wouldn't give anything away. "Once we get it authenticated, we'll put it up for sale."

He nodded. "The smart thing to do, of course, if you're not a collector."

I turned back toward him. "No. I'm afraid that our mother's Austen mania didn't quite rub off." I glanced around the room. "Maybe you might be interested in the diary?"

A private sale would be much easier, quicker too, but first I would have to convince Ellen. I'd also have to figure out a way to tell her that I'd done what she'd explicitly told me not to do—reveal the existence of the diary.

"I'm not sure if I'm in the market for more Austenalia."

"Oh." I had thought he'd be very interested. "Don't mention it to anyone, okay?" I said to Ethan. "Ellen's afraid of it disappearing before we figure out what to do with it."

He smiled. "I wouldn't dream of it. I wouldn't get your hopes up though. Most of these things turn out to be well-meant forgeries or hoaxes. But I'd be glad to take a look at it for you." He moved toward me and then put an arm around my shoulders. "Shall we finish the tour?"

We eventually came to a stop in what I supposed one would call the conservatory. The glass walls and ceilings housed a sea of plants, which in turn encased a comfortable-looking wicker sofa piled high with cushions, along with several matching chairs.

"This would be amazing when it rains." I could imagine lying on the sofa, looking up at the ceiling and watching the raindrops as they splattered against the glass.

"Yes, I suppose it would. I hadn't thought about it."

"You should try it sometime."

"Perhaps I will." He took me in his arms again, and I didn't resist. To be honest, I had to restrain myself from flinging myself at him.

"You're a very special girl, Mimi," he said.

"No, not really. I'm very ordinary." I knew from experience that the surest way to get a man to repeat a compliment was to deflect it on the first try.

"Let's test that theory." He leaned forward and placed his lips against mine. Softly. With just a light pressure. Oh dear, he was good.

I'd meant to be a little more coy. After all, I'd leaped into his car and come to his house late at night, which I'm pretty sure would give most guys the wrong idea, whichever side of the pond they lived on. But he was such a good kisser, and I was so lost in the fantasy of the moment. A handsome, rich British gentleman wanted to romance me, and I intended to let him. Well, for a few minutes, anyway. I might be infatuated, but I wasn't a complete idiot.

❦❦❦❦❦

Mimi didn't come home until well after midnight. I was livid. I wasn't my sister's keeper. Not technically, anyway. I knew she was with Ethan, but that only made me more worried. At least she'd told someone where she was going, although I wish it hadn't been Tom Braddock. The poor man had gone a little gray around the mouth when I asked if he'd seen her. I was sure

Mimi's choice of messenger was deliberate. She wanted Tom to be very clear on where he stood, which was nowhere in her vicinity.

I heard a car motor outside. The drive into the stable block was on the opposite side of the courtyard from the open doors, and the engine purred softly. Expensively.

I crossed the room to the single, small window in the bathroom. Carefully, I lifted the blinds and peered out in time to see Mimi climbing out of a black sports car.

She was a grown-up, but she was still my sister, and I was disappointed in her. I knew that she was growing desperate. Age and money seemed to be the twin ghosts nipping at her heels these days, but I still found it painful to watch.

Ethan walked her to her door. Her room was across the courtyard from mine, so I had a clear view as he kissed her and then turned back to his car. I saw the quick, wistful glance Mimi cast over her shoulder at him as he drove away, and then she opened her door with the key card and disappeared.

It wouldn't last. It never did. I would have given anything if Mimi would open her eyes for a change and truly see the man she'd set her sights on. But we were grown-ups now, and I could no longer hope that she would change. Mimi was who she was. I loved her. She was my sister, after all. But that didn't make her self-defeating choices any easier to watch.

Even after Mimi returned, I spent a restless night fretting about Daniel, Mrs. Parrot, and the mystery of the diary. As the sky lightened, I took Cassandra's diary from my bedside table and slipped out through the French doors onto the small patio. With only the birds for company, I settled into a wooden chair and flipped back through the pages of old-fashioned handwriting.

Jane still nurses a tendre for Jack Smith, which dismays our mother enormously. He is the natural son of a gentleman, or so we have been told, but he has no fortune and few prospects. At least he has been provided with an education, but none of us knows what will become of him when he leaves Steventon.

I have discouraged her, of course, in her affection for him. I even went so far as to urge my father to send her to London or to my uncle's house, but he does not heed my warning. None of them knows that Jack returns her feelings, for she confides in no one but me, and Jack confides in no one.

Jane will be <u>along</u> *presently, however much she may resent my interference.* <u>The</u> *cough I brought back from Steventon tickles my throat. Jane advises a more* <u>narrow</u> *course of rest than I would like. She brings hot water for a compress for my chest. It is the* <u>way</u> *of the world, I suppose. How could* <u>it</u> *be otherwise? When the sun shines, sickness* <u>goes</u> *indoors to escape the cleansing work of nature.*

Some of the words were underlined. Very odd. I checked the dates of the entries, which seemed very sporadic. Cassandra obviously hadn't made a point of writing in the diary on a regular basis.

She'd clearly been quite concerned about Jane's feelings for this Jack Smith, though, just as I was fretting about Mimi's fascination with Ethan.

Was Jane's attachment to Jack Smith common knowledge? I didn't remember ever hearing his name, but I was no expert. What if this was new information? How valuable would that make it? I closed the diary and laid a hand on top of the cover.

Daniel could help me. After all, wasn't that why he was here? I thought of the conversation I'd overheard at the Vyne the previous afternoon, a man's murmured reply to Mrs. Parrot. Could it have been Daniel? Was he what he seemed, or was he, too, after the diary, as I suspected Mrs. Parrot must be?

The sun had risen enough so that it was faintly visible on the eastern horizon. I watched the dawn bloom into fullness and stayed where I was, my hand on the diary, my gaze on the line of trees across the way.

I dare you to make a happy ending out of this mess, Jane Austen.

Talking to myself, or more specifically to a long-dead author, wasn't going to get me anywhere. Time for a shower and a strong cup of tea, because the new day that awaited was likely to be as complicated as it would be long.

imi didn't appear at break-
fast that morning. Tom
joined us a few minutes
later, and I noticed he had
dark circles under his eyes. When Mrs. Parrot entered the dining room, she also appeared a little worse for the wear. She had
painted an extra layer of rouge on her cheeks, which clashed
with her orange hair.

Ethan was the last one to arrive. He was staying at his own
house but eating his meals with us.

He pulled up a chair to the end of the table where I sat.
"Mind if I join you?" he asked.

What could I possibly say? No, because you've been ruining
my sister's reputation?

"Please do." I forced myself to make conversation. "Are
you looking forward to today's walk? You've probably already
been to Chawton Cottage."

"I think each time I visit there is like the first." His smile was almost dreamy. "This is turning out to be a week of firsts."

I paused and bit my lip. Was it possible I had misjudged him? Maybe he really liked my sister. Maybe he had fallen for her.

A waiter appeared to take our order for the hot breakfast, and Ethan ordered the full English. I contented myself with poached eggs and toast.

"You and Mimi seem to have hit it off," I said, forgoing the subtle approach.

He nodded and sipped his coffee. "Quite."

"Ethan—"

He set his cup down and fiddled with the handle. "I know you're concerned about your sister, but let me assure you—"

"I'm sorry. It's none of my business, obviously." I was not going to meddle. I was not going to be the reincarnation of my mother. "It's just that she's vulnerable at the moment."

"I understand. Losing your mother must have been very difficult for both of you. Mimi said she's ready to begin a new chapter in her life."

She was? That was news to me.

"And you?" I asked. "Will you live in Hampshire full-time now that you have a home here?"

"No, no. I'm a Londoner born and bred. This will be my base at weekends though."

Obviously I should have gone into whatever Ethan did for a living. "So not a new start then."

"Well, not in terms of living arrangements."

"So what's this new life Mimi's about to start?" I asked him. "A sister is always the last to know."

Ethan looked a bit uncomfortable. "Perhaps she would rather tell you herself. She did say that your mother's legacy would allow her to start a new venture. One she's dreamed of for some time." He frowned. "But surely you know that."

"You mean her store?" She'd talked about it for years, quitting her job with the large department-store chain in Atlanta and opening up her own boutique. "Yes, I guess it's possible she might—"

"I'd say with that sort of money, it's a great deal more than possible."

"What sort of money?"

Now Ethan looked very uncomfortable. "I don't normally discuss personal finances, but Mimi was very . . . forthcoming last night. About the value of . . . your mother's estate, if you see what I mean."

Oh, I saw what he meant, all right. Our mother's modest estate had clearly taken on more epic proportions when she'd talked of it with Ethan. Mom only had a little in savings, and the house wasn't worth all that much, but that obviously wasn't the message Ethan received.

"I'm afraid Mimi's expectations may be a bit . . . grandiose."

Ethan's fingers stilled on the handle of his coffee cup. "In what way?"

"What my mother left us might be enough for Mimi to make a start on her dream, but as for any kind of significant financial backing . . . " I shook my head. "I think Mimi sometimes wishes things into more than they are."

Ethan's expression didn't change, but the air around him crackled with a strange sort of tension. Disappointment, almost.

What had I done? He'd believed Mimi to be some sort of heiress, obviously. The news that she was what she'd always been—a professional woman of average means—was clearly unwelcome.

"So she's not about to lay the foundation for the next great American clothing empire?"

"Mimi?" I said in surprise, and then I felt ashamed of my disloyalty. "Well, you never know. But there's a lot of work—and luck—between here and there."

Ethan's expression was now well and truly shuttered, and guilt took up residence in my stomach next to the poached eggs and toast. I hadn't meant to expose Mimi's fraud, but would she understand that? On the other hand, I wasn't too sorry that I'd done it. If Ethan only liked her because he thought she might be a possible meal ticket, then she was better off without him.

❧❧❧❧❧

If it hadn't been for my stupid blisters, I could have hiked circles around Ellen, a fact that filled me with satisfaction. But I did have the blisters, and when I slipped on my hiking boots that morning, I almost burst into tears. I limped into the reception foyer in the nick of time. Tom was counting people and starting to frown. Ethan was already there, looking gorgeous in a rough-hewn kind of way. The outdoorsy look suited him, a look that most businessmen I'd known couldn't have pulled off.

I slipped past the others, all chatting enthusiastically about the day's pilgrimage to Jane Austen's House Museum, and stood next to Ethan.

"Good morning."

"Hello, Mimi."

Hmm. Not a very enthusiastic greeting.

"Thank you again for last night." Good manners were always the right way to go, weren't they?

"My pleasure." He barely smiled, and he sounded like one of the hotel staff.

"I'm looking forward to seeing Jane Austen's house today." I was never one to give up easily.

"Yes, of course," he said, and then nodded and walked away toward the front door.

Tom urged us out to the waiting vehicles. I tried to hang back so I could see which one Ethan would choose without looking too obvious. Only Ethan seemed indecisive, and before I knew it, Tom was asking if I'd sit in the very back of the tour company van. "Since you're one of our smaller women," he said with a smile.

I could hardly argue with or be offended by his remark. Didn't every woman want to be considered thin? I climbed into the back of the van and found myself squashed between

Karen, the television producer, and another woman whose name I couldn't remember. I glanced out the window and saw Ethan climbing into the taxi.

Ellen somehow managed to score the front passenger seat in our van. She and Tom were laughing about something as we moved off down the driveway of Oakley Hall. Only then did I get my first hint of motion sickness.

The journey to Upper Farringdon took half an hour and involved enough curves and twists in the road to leave me green by the time we got there. I stumbled out of the van, but Tom caught my upper arm and steadied me. I flashed him a grateful smile, but then regretted it almost immediately when he returned my smile with a very happy one of his own.

We'd stopped outside the church in the little village. I wanted to ask if I could run in and use the restroom, but no one else seemed to have the same need, so I kept my mouth shut. I was determined not to be the princess of the group, however much I might actually be the princess of the group.

Across the road from the church, a small whitewashed cottage with a thatched roof boasted the most beautiful bank of climbing roses I'd ever seen. I stepped across the road to admire them and, much to my delight, Ethan joined me.

"It's like something out of a fairy tale," I said. "So peaceful. Like nothing bad could ever happen there."

"You think it's charmed?"

"Well, if not charmed, then definitely charming."

He laughed just enough to relieve my anxiety. "Nicely said."

Tom called out to us then, and we returned across the road to join the group.

"From here, it's three miles to Chawton," he said. "We'll only have a limited amount of time at the Austen cottage, I'm afraid. About twenty minutes or so. Then we'll walk back here by a different route and enjoy lunch at the pub we saw when we came through the village." His eyes twinkled, which was charming in the same way as the cottage—old-fashioned and unthreatening.

The group set off behind Tom, and I fell into step with Ethan, who had gotten over whatever moodiness had been bothering him earlier. Ellen shot me a disapproving look, of course, but I was too happy with the company and with the scenery to pay much attention to her.

We left the little village and took a gravel road along a ridge that gave an open view of the green valley, dotted with cottages. Not all of them were as pretty as the little one by the church, but the whole scene was as picturesque as any tourist could hope for.

Ethan and I talked, but not about anything earth-shattering. I simply enjoyed being in his company. We seemed to have a lot in common. He liked to travel. I did too, although most of my travel was for work. He preferred literary fiction, and I said that was my choice as well. I didn't say that I didn't actually read much of it, only that it was what I enjoyed. We talked about the theater—I traveled to New York City often enough that I could keep up my end of that conversation. Besides, I really did enjoy the theater. I usually only went, though, when my company treated us to an evening out during a buying trip.

I hustled along beside Ethan and tried to keep from wincing. We reached the end of the gravel road, crossed a paved lane, and set out along the edge of a field. The grain—wheat, I think—was knee high and mossy green. I wondered how long it would be before it turned golden in the sun. The field stretched to another line of trees several hundred yards away, and I knew the golden grain against the crystalline blue sky would be breathtaking.

Once past the field, Tom led us onto a narrow dirt lane. By that time, my blisters were screamingly painful. I'd fallen behind Ethan and into the company of my sister. We didn't speak. I concentrated on putting one foot in front of the other. I had no clue what she might be thinking about.

I found out soon enough.

"You're making a fool of yourself," she said quietly as we moved into the shade where the footpath merged with the lane.

"In your opinion." Heaven knew she had plenty of them.

"At least don't be so obvious. You're following him around like a puppy."

That one stung. "I am not. We weren't even in the same van on the way over."

"Well, that wasn't for lack of effort on your part."

The problem with sisters is that they know all your tricks.

"It's mutual," I insisted.

The group had stopped, and we moved to stand a little apart from everyone, resting in the shade. I slid off my small backpack and took the water bottle from its exterior pocket. I took a long drink and wiped my forehead with the back of my hand. It was already hot and steamy, and it was barely past ten o'clock.

"I'm not cleaning up any messes, Mimi. I swear."

"Message received, Ell. Loud and clear." I twisted the cap back onto my bottle and stepped away from her before I said something I would regret. Although at this point, that list was so long, an addition to it could hardly matter.

"I have a bit of a surprise for everyone," Tom announced, and then we heard a jangling of metal and the clip of hooves against the hard-packed dirt lane. I looked up to see a horse-drawn carriage moving toward us.

"We've seen what foot travel was like in Jane Austen's day. We're grateful for dry weather and dry roads, aren't we?" Tom asked. The Austenites nodded in unison. "I thought you might like to get a sense of what traveling in a carriage feels like."

The Austenites laughed and hooted with approval when the conveyance pulled up next to us. Tom clearly knew how to keep his clientele happy. The driver was even dressed in period costume, complete with a top hat.

"We'll have to go in shifts," Tom said. "Just to the end of the lane, about half a mile down." He motioned to Ellen and me. "Ladies, would you like to give it a try?"

I had to get Ethan to join me in the carriage. I hated to let that opportunity for romance slip by unclaimed. This was far better than a ride in Central Park. I maneuvered carefully, and to my delight, Ethan wound up in the carriage with us, although Ellen sat next to me and he sat opposite us, wedged into the seat with one of the married couples.

"There you go." Tom closed the door and nodded to the driver. "Just wait for us at the other end of the lane." And then we were off.

The driver flicked the reins, and the horse began to move. It wasn't my first time in a carriage, but this was different. Maybe it was the secluded country lane where the tree branches arched so high overhead that they formed a tunnel. Maybe it was having Ethan facing me, flashing a smile from time to time. Or perhaps it was simply the Austen-inspired moment. I imagined that the road and the woods couldn't look much different than they would have two hundred years ago.

The carriage had pretty good shock absorbers, or whatever they called them in the old days. We flowed along with barely the occasional bump or jostle. I turned to look at Ellen, only to find her smiling back at me, and we exchanged a look of delight. It was a rare moment of mutual joy in our relationship.

All too soon, we reached the other end of the lane. Ethan hopped down from the carriage and offered me his hand, which I gladly took. I felt a zing worthy of a full-fledged Austen heroine, but then he let go and offered his hand to Ellen, who was scrambling from the carriage behind me. I stepped to the side of the road to give the others room to find their footing. It didn't take long before the carriage was empty and the driver took off on his return trip. The five of us were left to stand in the shade and make conversation.

"Will you stay at the museum and take the van back to lunch, or will you keep walking?" I said to Ethan. I didn't realize until I asked the question that it sounded a bit like I was trying to find out his plans so I could follow them. Oops. "I'm going to walk myself," I said, even though my feet would have far preferred the other option. Ethan could call the next shot. If he wanted to spend time with me, he would choose to keep walking as well.

"I'm not sure," he said. "I think I'll see how I'm feeling when we get there."

"Have you been to the museum before?"

He nodded. "Several times. But I'm keen to see the new visitors' center. They've also recently refurbished the kitchen to its original state."

"Oh."

Frankly, I couldn't have cared less about the kitchen or the visitors' center, but if it meant time with Ethan, I could manufacture some interest.

"But you came here to walk," he said with a kind smile. "I wouldn't want to interfere with that."

Ouch. If he'd really wanted to spend time with me, he would have interfered up one side and down the other.

"To each his own," I chirped. Like a bird, I chirped. It even nauseated *me*. I felt as if I had been riding in the back of the tour-company minivan.

What had happened to our easy camaraderie of the night before? He was certainly still pleasant, but that connection, that feeling of having known him forever... well, it had vanished almost as quickly as it had developed. Almost as if it had been a dream.

I moved closer to Ellen and left him to chat with the other three.

"What?" she said. "I thought the whole point was to cozy up to Ethan."

"Don't be mean." My throat grew tight, and tears threatened to spill over. I was so tired, and not just physically. I was sore too, and I wasn't just talking about my blisters. I'd spent so many years trying to find Mr. Right that I had battle fatigue, or whatever the romantic equivalent of it was.

"Sorry." And she was, I could see. "Do you have enough water?"

I nodded and then turned to face the field, as if I were admiring the view.

"He's not worth it, Meems." The old nickname was nearly my undoing.

"That's the problem, Ell. He is worth it."

She shook her head. I could see that much out of the corner of my eye. "Someday, you'll learn."

"Someday, so will you." But I at least managed to accompany the words with the hint of a smile. "Do you see the rest of them yet?"

"They'll be here any moment. In the meantime, we'll just stand over here and talk."

For most of my life, I had despised being indebted to my sister, but now I was simply grateful for her presence. And her kindness.

"That would be nice," I said, and to my surprise, I found that I meant it.

CHAPTER

ELEVEN

fter the carriage ride, I left Mimi to walk with some of the others and stayed behind with Daniel. We passed through a succession of fields that rolled gently over the surrounding countryside. We had made it to the other side of the open space when I faced my first real obstacle of the walking tour.

This stile was seriously daunting. Stinging nettles lurked on either side of it. I made a face at the rickety contraption, took a deep breath, and prepared to conquer it on my own. I made it up the first two steps, but the third one stymied me. And then I saw the hand stretched out toward me. Daniel's hand. He stood beside me and smiled with encouragement.

"I know, I know," he said. "You're perfectly capable. But maybe just once you can let me give you a hand."

I looked down at the ground from my perch, and dizziness overcame me. Instinctively, I reached for him, and he steadied me.

"Breathe," he said, and I complied.

"I think I'm stuck." I hadn't meant to say the words out loud. I never admitted weakness to anyone other than myself.

"No. You're just resting." I could hear the smile in his voice.

"It's not funny."

"Of course not."

I looked at him, and he was grinning at me. "You're enjoying this, aren't you?"

The smile moved to his eyes, which lit with glee. "Absolutely."

That was all the challenge I needed. "Here I go." I lifted one foot, swung it over the top of the fence, and found my footing on the other side. Now came the hard part. I had to swivel so that I faced the direction from which we'd come, maintain my balance on that one precariously placed foot, swing my other leg over the fence, and then find the step below with that foot.

"You've got this," Daniel said.

"Here goes nothing." I gripped his hand, flung my other leg over the fence, and prayed my foot would hit the four-inch-wide board that served as a middle step.

My boot scraped the wood, and I teetered in midair for one very long moment, but then Daniel moved our hands so that I could regain my balance, and my foot caught hold. I clambered down the remaining step and was grateful to find myself on solid ground once more.

"See?" He stepped up to the stile and practically vaulted over it. "Nothing to it."

"Easy for you to say." We moved away so that the others could take their turns climbing over.

"But you did it."

I smiled at him. I couldn't help myself. No matter how many years had passed, we still had that easy camaraderie that sucked me in every time.

"Come on," he said. "Let's walk to the end of the path. The others will catch up."

We had emerged from a field alongside someone's backyard. A trampoline and a child-sized version of a marquee dominated the fenced yard.

"Some things are universal, huh?" Daniel said, following my gaze. "My girls beg me for a trampoline on a regular basis, but I won't get them one."

"Why not?"

"Do you know how much a pediatric orthopedist costs?"

I laughed, and then we moved along in companionable silence, skirting the house and emerging into a very ordinary cul-de-sac. "Look, Dan. It's the suburbs."

A ring of brick homes, taller than my brick ranch back in Dallas but still with a cookie-cutter sameness to them, testified to the ordinariness of the street. We waited there for the rest of the group, and then Tom led us to the connecting road. Across the street was a large, open park.

"That belongs to Chawton Great House," Tom said. "We'll be visiting there this afternoon. It was owned by Jane Austen's brother Edward, who was adopted into a wealthy family."

We made our way up the street past more quaint cottages and beautiful gardens. "Look." Daniel pointed to a plain, square brick house that stood thirty yards in front of us at a junction in the road. "That's it."

"That's what?"

"That's Chawton Cottage. Jane Austen's House Museum."

I wasn't sure what I was expecting, but this ordinary structure wasn't it. The large house sat practically on top of the road, and an irregular pattern in the brick showed where a large front window had been filled in. Where were the climbing roses? The charming thatched roof? This was a solid bulwark against the weather, not the graceful home I'd imagined.

We moved closer, and Tom gathered us on the sidewalk opposite the house in front of a tea room that bore the sign Cassandra's Cup. The garden to the left of the cottage was gorgeous, to be sure, and whoever ran the place obviously did so with a great deal of care. But I'd expected Jane Austen's home to be more . . . romantic.

"As I said earlier," Tom continued, "we only have twenty minutes or so before we need to set out on the second part of our walk. Otherwise we'll be late for lunch. For those of you who would like to stay longer, Mrs. Parrot will be here in an hour with the van. She will drive you back to Upper Farringdon to the pub."

"C'mon," Daniel said. "Let's check out the holy ground."

The visitors' center was in the small stable block to the right of the cottage. We decided to forgo the introductory video and the peek into the bake house. Signs led us in a loop around the back of the cottage to the visitors' entrance on the far side. Here we found the separate kitchen where the Austen ladies and their servants had prepared their meals. It was attached to the house, but there was no door leading into the rest of the interior.

"I bet that was a pain in bad weather," I said, envisioning the Austens' maid-of-all-work ferrying a soup tureen out the kitchen door and into the adjacent side entrance in the midst of a gale.

We followed the route of my imaginary maid and found ourselves in the sitting room of the cottage. It was about the same size as my living room at home and contained, among other things, a piano from the period.

We crossed the vestibule, and there was the dining room. Again, it was about the same size as mine at home. By the window stood a small table and chair. The table had a plastic shield around it.

"What's that?" Daniel asked.

"My mother used to talk about this. The holy of holies. That's the table where Jane wrote most of her novels." It was about eighteen inches in diameter and looked more decorative than functional. At home, I would have put a potted plant on it.

"Not very impressive," Daniel said in a low voice. "Why the Plexiglas?"

That much I also knew from my mother. "So that all the devoted Austenites won't rub their hands all over it."

"Really?" He looked at me as if he thought I was joking.

"Really," I said with a wink.

After that, we made our way upstairs. I felt a small pang that my mother wasn't there to see this with me. "Here's her bedroom." Daniel nodded to the left as we reached the top of the stairs.

Again, it was a normal-sized room, rather low-ceilinged, with a fireplace and exposed wooden beams overhead. Two cupboards occupied recesses on either side of the fireplace. The room contained a small canopied bed and a chair.

Daniel looked down at one of the information placards. "It says she shared this room with her sister." He looked up in surprise. "You'd think with a house this size, they would have had separate bedrooms."

I eyed the rather narrow bed. It was bigger than a twin, but hardly big enough to be considered a double in American terms. "No wonder they were so close, if they had to share that."

I knew that I was being snarky. It was more than likely my way of holding this whole experience at arm's length. Seeing Jane Austen's home made me miss my mother with an intensity that I'd thought had abated over the past couple of months. She should have been standing here with me.

"Ellen? Are you okay?" Daniel asked.

"Yes, yes. I'm fine." But I wasn't. I'd have sat down in the chair if it hadn't had a dainty little nosegay of lavender wrapped in ribbon on the seat. It was a very genteel way of discouraging visitors from collapsing on the antiques.

"I don't think you are." He took my elbow. "Do you need some fresh air?"

"That's probably a good idea." My vision blurred, and I felt off-balance, but I refused to faint in Jane Austen's bedroom.

Daniel helped me down the stairs and back outside. He led me to a bench under an enormous tree in the garden. The shade felt wonderful. He pulled the water bottle from my pack and pressed it into my hands.

"Drink," he ordered.

I was only too glad to oblige. "I'm sorry. I don't mean to be weird."

He was quiet for a long moment. "It's your mom, huh?"

His gentle question popped the cork that had been holding back my bottled emotions. I burst into tears. At least the other visitors would think I was just an Austen nut overcome by the experience of being in her house.

I retrieved a tissue from my pack and wiped my eyes. "I wasn't expecting this."

"Why not? I would have been."

"I just didn't think . . . I'm only here because my mom made me come. I don't really care about all these Jane Austen sites."

"But you do care about your mom. I remember how obsessed she was. When we were in college, she kept telling me I looked just like she imagined Mr. Darcy would."

I cringed. "She didn't."

"Oh, she did."

That, at least, made me smile. "I guess it just hit me that I'm here to say good-bye to her."

"Which was what she wanted."

"I'm not sure what she wanted. I thought it was for Mimi and me to form some kind of bond." Not to mention deal with that stupid diary.

"Maybe your mom didn't have that detailed an agenda. Maybe she just wanted the two of you to see why she loved Jane Austen, and each of you, so much."

"Maybe." At least our conversation had stemmed my tears.

"Did you want to see the rest of the house?" He glanced at his watch. "We need to find Tom if we're going to do the second half of the walk."

"It's okay." I picked up my backpack and stood up. "I think I've seen what I needed to see."

Daniel looked down at me, concern etched into the lines around his eyes and mouth. "Ellen . . . "

"Yes?"

"Would you have dinner with me tonight?"

I wasn't ready for this. I so wasn't ready for this. I didn't even know if I could really trust Daniel, and I certainly didn't know if I could trust myself.

I gave him a faint smile. "I don't think we get to pick where we're sitting. Tom mentioned using place cards to kind of mix things up."

"No, I don't mean with the group. I mean just you and me. I'll get the kitchen at the hotel to fix us a picnic."

"Can we do that?"

He smiled softly. "Given what we've paid to be on this trip, I think we can do whatever we want."

"But Tom has someone coming to sing Jane Austen–era music."

"I think he'll understand. I'll speak to him."

I'd run out of excuses, except for the ones that really mattered. I looked into Daniel's eyes. He'd been a kind and helpful companion all morning. He hadn't pressed me at all about the diary, leaving any discussion up to me. What would it hurt to spend time alone with him? I wasn't a gullible college freshman who was going to fall for the first good-looking guy she met.

"Okay." I surprised myself with the answer.

"Great," he said. "I'll make the arrangements."

"Look. There's Tom on the sidewalk." We could see him across the street with a few members of the group gathering around him.

"Time to go," Daniel said. We walked back through the visitors' center and across the road. I cast one last glance back at the cottage.

"Do you think she would mind?" I asked Daniel. "All those people tromping through her house all day long?"

He patted my shoulder. "I think she'd be proud of all the happiness she's brought to people. Isn't that what we want to be remembered for, in the end?"

"I guess so." But I had to wonder: Was it enough simply to make others happy? Or should our lives leave some other lasting mark?

My mother's death left me distinctly aware of my own mortality, but Daniel's words made me wonder: What would I leave behind when my time came? At the moment, not much. That sobering thought was enough to keep me quiet as we made our way back across the street to find Tom.

managed to paste a smile on my face and walk beside Daniel to Upper Farringdon without any further outbursts. After lunch at the charming pub, we returned to Chawton to tour the Great House. The stately home was now a center for the study of early women's writing and so served more as a library than a tourist attraction. If we hadn't been with Tom and the tour company, we'd never have gotten inside, since it wasn't open to the public.

We were asked to leave our packs in the office while we toured the house. It was decorated in a mixture of styles but was still strongly influenced by the original Jacobean structure. Dark wood paneling, tapestries, and mullioned windows gave it more of an Elizabethan than a Regency feel, and Jane and Cassandra would have dined there frequently when their brother was in residence. Just as the enormity of the Vyne had made me wonder how the sisters felt about the size of their house compared to it,

I wondered now if they minded that their brother had put them in a cottage while he and his family lived in such splendor.

Daniel gave me some space on this tour and walked with the others, leaving me on my own. It felt strangely empty to move through the dark hallways and paneled rooms alone. I'd fought my feelings for him from the moment I came across him on the path outside Oakley Hall. Now, though, I realized that I was tired of fighting. I wasn't ready to surrender, but maybe I could relax just a little.

❧❧❧❧❧

Ellen was acting strangely, so I avoided her. I wasn't being a very good sister by Austen standards, certainly not up to the devotion of the Dashwoods in *Sense and Sensibility*, but I was preoccupied with figuring out why Ethan ran so hot and cold. One minute he was flirting with me and taking me to his house, and the next he seemed indifferent or vaguely tolerant. After the tour of Chawton Great House, I was glad to be out in the open air again, even if the sun was wreaking havoc with my complexion. I'd slathered on sunblock for sensitive skin and donned the baseball cap that Tom had found in the back of the van. I hoped no one would want it back, because at the rate I was perspiring, it would be pretty revolting in a matter of minutes.

Tom didn't seem to mind my sweat though. He walked beside me as the groundskeeper or gardener or whoever he was led us across a pasture liberally strewn with horse manure.

"Picturesque," I murmured under my breath. I didn't mean for Tom to hear me, but he laughed.

"That's one word for it."

I looked up at him. He really was a very nice man. He'd rescued me at lunch, when Ethan very deliberately moved away from the table where I'd been sitting. Tom hadn't hesitated to pull up a chair and join me. I'd acted as nonchalant as I could, but I was crushed by Ethan's on-again, off-again actions. What did he want from me? I wasn't a mind reader.

With Tom, no mind reading was necessary. We'd had a very pleasant chat, and he'd told me stories about the time he was stationed in a remote northern location, one that he wasn't allowed to name. He told tales of frozen pipes, long underwear, and growing a beard so his cheeks wouldn't freeze, and it made me almost glad for the summer heat. It could definitely have been worse.

The gardener at the Great House didn't believe in dawdling, and we soon found ourselves at the back of the group.

"You okay?" Tom asked.

"Don't fuss," I said, but I smiled. "I'm stronger than I look." Men tended to think that blonde curls meant not only a low IQ but physical inferiority as well.

"I don't doubt that."

"People always think I need special treatment."

"People like men? Or people like your sister?"

I shouldn't have been surprised at his perceptiveness. "Both, actually."

"I'll try not to be one of them." But it went against his nature, I could tell, not to watch over me. I didn't know whether it was because of his military background, his old-school conditioning as a gentleman, or his interest in me. Or all three.

Still, Tom was as easy to walk with as he was to talk to. I had to pause a couple of times on the uphill bits to catch my breath, and Tom stood quietly beside me, taking in the surroundings with a patient gaze.

"Are you glad for a break from herding us all around?" I asked him when we came to a stop at the bottom of a hill. We'd emerged from a short portion of trail under the trees into the blaze of the afternoon sun.

He shrugged. "I like being in charge, so it's really not an issue." He wasn't being vain, I could tell. Just honest.

"It's nice having a break from work," I said. "If nothing else, I've gotten that much from the trip."

He turned to me with a smile. "I hope you've gotten more than that."

"Oh, I didn't mean that the tour—" I blushed.

"I know. Sorry. Just teasing." His eyes sparkled in a very attractive way.

We started off again and caught up with the others as we made our way around the back of the Great House. We crossed through a line of trees at the top of the ridge, and the path became overgrown.

Tom looked back over his shoulder. "Watch out for the—"

"Ouch."

"Nettles." He reached for my arm where the vicious little brutes had attacked me.

"That hurts."

"Don't sound so surprised. I warned you yesterday."

"Yes, but I didn't expect it to be this bad." My skin burned like fire.

"Hang on." Tom stepped to the side of the path and looked around. Then he reached out and plucked a couple of dark green leaves. "Use these."

I eyed them with suspicion. "What are they?"

"Dockweed." He reached out and rubbed them vigorously on my reddening arm. Almost instantly, the pain disappeared.

"Thank you. Although I'm not sure there's actually anything in these leaves. I think it's just the rubbing."

He chuckled. "Either way, it helps."

It did, thank goodness. "Much better." The stinging died down. The redness too. "You always seem to be coming to my rescue."

The others had moved into the next meadow, and we were alone. Tom stood awfully close, and I felt a strange twist of anticipation in my midsection. That was silly, of course. He was just Tom.

"Mimi . . . " He reached out and took my hand in his. I was too surprised to protest.

"Do you ever let anyone see the real you?" Then, to my unexpected disappointment, he dropped his hand. Only why should I have been disappointed? I wasn't trying to encourage him.

"I don't know what you m—"

He kissed me. Out of the blue, didn't-see-it-coming, full-on kissing. He was pretty good at it too. The problem was, he wasn't Ethan, and I had never meant for this to happen.

I stepped back before either of us could get carried away. "Tom—"

"I'm sorry." He ran his fingers through his hair. "That was unprofessional." He looked truly distraught, and my heart went out to him.

"Don't worry about it. Really. It's okay."

"It's not, but you're nice to say so." He paused, swallowed. "I don't want to make you feel . . . uncomfortable."

He really was too nice a man for me to let him twist in the wind. "It's okay. Really. Besides, it's always nice to be admired. It's just that I don't—" I didn't want to hurt his feelings. "I mean, I don't think it's a great idea." Although the jelly in my knees might have said otherwise, if I'd let it do the talking.

"I guess not. I am sorry."

I hated that he was so distressed, but I hated even more that I was. I would never have expected that. "Why don't we catch up with the others?" I kept my tone bright. "As for this"—I waved a hand—"I won't tell if you won't." I shot him my best girlie smile. "You know what they say. What happens at Chawton Great House stays at Chawton Great House."

His shoulders relaxed, and he looked relieved but also a little sad. I didn't want him to look sad. I'd experienced enough sadness, caused enough sadness even, in the past year without distressing a perfectly nice man like Tom Braddock.

"I think the gardener mentioned something about roses?" I slipped past Tom and took a few steps down the trail.

Thankfully, he followed without any further apologies. With any luck, he'd let it go, just as we'd agreed. I tried to refocus my mind on Ethan. A week wasn't very long to build some sort of a relationship with him. I needed to stay focused on my goal, because I couldn't afford to be distracted by relationships that were never going to go anywhere or by men who didn't fit the bill.

I kept telling myself that, but it didn't make it any easier to forget that kiss. And I wasn't sure what bothered me more—that I'd enjoyed it more than I should have or that Tom had jumped straight to remorse afterward.

CHAPTER
THIRTEEN

hile we'd been tour-
ing Chawton that day,
Mrs. Parrot had over-
seen the transfer of our
luggage from Oakley Hall to our new hotel at Langrish. I could
only hope that no bellman had slipped a disk trying to lift Mimi's
monstrosity. I had made a point that morning of putting the
diary into my daypack. No way would I trust it in a suitcase that
would be under anyone's supervision but my own.

The new hotel was more secluded and less glamorous than
Oakley Hall, but it also had a certain careless charm. Whereas
Oakley Hall had been square and elegant, Langrish Hall rambled a bit, with distinct sections brought together by the use of
the same native gray stone. The hotel was nestled among the
small hills, the perfect place to escape from everyday life.

I made the mistake of telling Mimi about my dinner plans
when we reached the hotel. She barely paused to unpack in her

room before she appeared in mine, ready to prep me for my big evening out.

I'm not the kind of woman who should be plucked and pruned, cosmetically speaking, except maybe pruned in a too-long-in-the-bathtub kind of way. I looked at Mimi's reflection in the bathroom mirror and marveled at how her perfect eyebrows had ever been created, much less maintained in all their arched beauty. Even with professional assistance, they couldn't have been easy to pull off. My own eyebrows were a disaster. I could never remember which part to pluck—above or below?—so I left them to grow unfettered in all their scrubby glory. I thought they looked normal, ordinary, like the rest of me. They weren't noticeably atrocious, except to my sister.

"That's what you're wearing?" Mimi had moved on from my eyebrows and was now scrutinizing my trusty blue dress with decided skepticism.

"I don't have anything else."

"You only brought one dress?"

"Yes. That's why I can lift my own luggage." I couldn't resist. She had it coming, with all the eyebrow scrutiny.

"Touché." She smiled. More perfection, of course, with whitened teeth and lipstick that had been outlined with a lip pencil. "Want to borrow one of my dresses?"

I was touched by the offer, actually. Mimi rarely—no, make that *never*—loaned out her clothes. But I couldn't see myself pulling off a dress like the strapless, pink number she'd worn to the welcome dinner.

"I think I'll just stick to Old Faithful." I'd felt fine about my dress until I saw it through my sister's eyes. Now all I could see were the wrinkles, the slight stain on the skirt, and the hemline that was a little short.

"At least let me do your makeup."

I sighed. "Okay, but you're not touching my hair."

In the end, she got her way with my hair too. As I left my room to meet Daniel, I still wore the plain blue dress, but my hair had been straightened into a sexy curtain that hung well below my shoulders. Really, it didn't even look like my hair. My eyes appeared bluer and a little mysterious, thanks to all the smoky eyeliner, and my lips glistened with pale pink gloss.

I made it as far as the lobby before I lost my courage. I slipped into the women's restroom, dampened a paper towel, and proceeded to remove most of my sister's handiwork. I might have been opening the door just a crack to Daniel, but I wasn't ready to fling it wide open.

He was waiting outside the hotel, carrying a picnic basket.

"I remembered how much you like picnics."

He really wasn't fighting fair, and I was doubly glad I had wiped off most of the makeup.

"Do you think we'll get in trouble for missing the evening program?" *Keep it light, Ellen. Keep it easy.*

"Only if Mrs. Parrot catches us." That familiar, beguiling grin. I'd never constructed any defenses against it in college, and I still didn't have any.

"Then we'd better get out of sight."

He laughed and nodded toward the path. "After you."

We made our way through the garden behind the hotel, and I was almost sorry to leave it. It was certainly gorgeous enough, and romantic enough, to have suited any purpose Daniel had in mind. Instead, he led me up a hillside, through a charming trellised gate, and in among the trees that dotted the slope, until we reached the ridge above.

Clouds were piling up in the distance. I realized I should have brought an umbrella. Usually I was much better at remembering such practical things, but something about Hampshire seemed to be undermining my natural organizational abilities.

"Sun or shade?" Daniel asked.

"Shade." The clouds were darker now, more ominous, and I didn't want to get caught in the rain completely unprotected. Agreeing to spend the evening with Daniel was risk enough for one day.

The view was spectacular, though, a panoramic vista straight out of a Jane Austen movie.

"How can anything possibly be so beautiful?" I said. I sank to the ground beneath the tree where he'd placed the picnic basket. The grass was cool and soft beneath me. "It's like that scene in *The Wizard of Oz*, where everything's in black and white before Dorothy opens the door to the farmhouse. But then she steps out into a whole new world that's so brilliant, it makes your eyes hurt."

"Technicolor." Daniel sat down next to me. "My mother said she saw that movie when she was young. First time she'd ever seen anything in color on the big screen. She said she cried, it was so beautiful."

He was looking at me with an intensity that set off warning bells in my head. But it also made my chest tighten and my pulse race. I was queasy and electric with excitement. Some reactions could never be tamed, even after more than fifteen years of separation.

I had to banish the intensity of the moment. "I guess that's why it's good to travel. See new places."

He reached out and laid his hand on mine where it rested on top of the grass. "Or maybe it's a good reason to revisit the past. Reclaim what you missed. What you didn't mean to leave behind."

I couldn't take it. I wasn't strong enough, even after all those years. I could either run away, revealing myself for the coward I was, or I could brazen it out, as if all of it was just a pleasant trip down memory lane.

"What's in that picnic basket? I'm starving." Daniel watched me quietly for a long moment and then leaned toward the wicker basket and undid the buckles. "Let's find out."

"How did you manage this, anyway?"

"My famous Edwards charm."

"Right."

"And a few extra pounds in the name of romance." He shrugged. "The chef is French."

"Good thinking. Sometimes it pays to be clever."

He laughed at my fairly weak joke, and I pretended that it was funny too.

I picked up one of the containers, opened it, and looked to Daniel for clarification.

"That would be the Cornish poached lobster with beluga mayonnaise." There was that devilish grin again.

"How long did it take you to memorize that?"

"Quite a while, given the chef's accent."

"And this?" I lifted the next container from the hamper.

"Some kind of foie gras. That one I couldn't remember if I tried."

I opened the last container and nearly fainted onto the grass. "Stilton and pears." I looked at him, and I had to bite my lip so that I wouldn't tear up. I'd been so strong, not showing any weakness, but I knew this might be my undoing. "You remembered."

"Are you kidding? Remember that time you made me drive around for an entire day in search of that stinky cheese?"

"You said it would have been easier to find weapons-grade plutonium."

"And I was right, wasn't I?"

That was the moment I let my guard down. I knew it. Daniel knew it. Even the picnic hamper probably knew it.

"Yes. You were right," I said.

He took out some utensils and began to transfer the food onto the china plates. "That's what I like to hear."

Wedgwood, silverware, sparkling water in tall champagne flutes. For once in my life, I decided not to be cautious. I wasn't going to analyze every look, every word. In short, I was going to act like my sister.

We ate in peace. Thunder rumbled in the distance, heralding a coming storm. I hadn't felt this relaxed in months. Not since the day my mother told me about her diagnosis.

"My mom would have loved this." I spoke the words without thinking.

The clouds cast shifting shadows on the crazy quilt of fields and hedgerows that stretched across the broad valley as far as I could see.

"But she sent you instead." Daniel studied me, his scrutiny a little too close for comfort.

"Yes." I set my plate aside and sipped the sparkling water. "That's the part I don't understand. She should have been the one on this tour. She could have come last year, even after her diagnosis. It wasn't until after the second round of chemo that she—"

No. I wasn't going to do this. I blinked hard. Swallowed.

"I'm sorry, Daniel. This is all so lovely, really. I don't mean to be a downer."

This time when he reached over and took my hand, he lifted it from my lap and laced his fingers through mine. The warm, simple contact was my undoing.

"Ellen . . . " He leaned over and very slowly, very softly, brushed his lips against mine. "I've missed you."

I didn't trust myself to speak, so instead I leaned toward him and kissed him back.

It wasn't a romantic kiss, really. Not in the traditional picnic-and-champagne kind of way. Instead, it was a kiss of regret. Longing. A ghost from the past.

"I'm glad you agreed to spend the evening with me," Daniel said as he pulled his lips away from mine. His face was so close. It wasn't the face I remembered, the face of the boy I had loved. Now it was the face of a man approaching middle age. Like my own, it had a few crow's feet around the eyes and some laugh lines around the mouth. His green eyes held knowledge and pain that hadn't been there when we were younger. He was still the Daniel I had known, but now he was much more.

"Have we changed too much?" he asked. "Am I an idiot to think I have a chance?"

No woman who has ever lived—anywhere, ever—could have resisted that. Not even me—sensible, practical Ellen Dodge.

"You're not an idiot," I said in a rather breathless voice.

Relief softened the lines around his eyes and mouth. "At least you're not dumping sparkling water on my head and telling me to get lost."

"Is that what you thought would happen?"

"I thought it was a possibility."

And then we were kissing again, and I felt as if I were still twenty. The years, the pain, the loneliness fell away. I had forgotten that anything could feel this good. This right.

And my eyebrows didn't matter. My dress didn't matter. What mattered was that I was here. Daniel was here. We had found that connection again. Had, in fact, taken it to a new level. An extraordinary level.

Eventually we came up for air, right before the raindrops started to fall. The air was thick with humidity and whatever electrical charges the distant lightning created.

"I have dessert," Daniel said. "But that might be redundant."

"Possibly. Unless it's chocolate."

"It is."

"Chocolate is never redundant."

"That's the girl I know and love." He meant it as a flip remark, but he froze and looked at me as if I might freak out. "Look, Ell, I'm not going to put any pressure on you."

I laughed. What else could I do? "I'd hate to see your definition of pressure. Following me to England. Stalking me at Jane Austen's birthplace. Romancing me with picnics and thunderstorms. But no pressure." I was teasing him, mostly. Mimi would have been proud of me. And Daniel hadn't mentioned the diary once. I'd obviously been worrying about nothing.

We sat under the sheltering branches of the tree while the rain fell, content with our chocolate and with getting to know each other all over again.

imi was still in my room when I got back. She'd clearly made herself at home. The bed was scattered with fashion magazines and the wrappers from the complimentary chocolates that the hotel had left on my pillow.

"Some things never change." I laughed as I scooped up the wrappers from the bed.

"Forget the chocolate." Mimi scrambled to her knees on the bed, her eyes shining like a child's at Christmas. "I want details."

I shouldn't have smiled. Mimi let out a whoop of laughter. "I knew it!"

"*Shh!*" It was late, and no doubt some of our fellow hikers were sound asleep.

"Only if you give me a detailed description of every single thing you ate, said, and did." She was like a kid in a candy store, but it wasn't because of the chocolates.

"We don't have time for that," I said, reaching for my daypack. "It's late. Let's get through as much of the diary as we can."

Mimi sighed. "You're such a party pooper. I want the scoop, not some dreary old diary entries about how many pence per yard muslin costs."

"You never know. There might be juicy, salacious gossip in here. It might be like a Regency version of the *National Enquirer*."

"I'd still rather hear about Daniel."

I rolled my eyes and joined her on the bed. "Do you want to read first, or should I?"

Mimi shook her head. "You start. I'll try to stay awake." She yawned.

"C'mon, Meems. We have to get through this. There may be something in here that Mom wanted us to see or to know. We have to figure out why she sent it to us."

"She sent it to you. You should figure it out."

"Just keep your eyes open and listen." I began to read.

Jane is too young to know her own mind. Why can she not see that? Jack has intelligence and manners to recommend him, but he is wild still and not to be relied upon. She will surely come to grief if she persists in this folly.

As we read, we found Cassandra's thoughts about Tom Lefroy, the man many people believed to be the love of Jane Austen's life. Cassandra, though, clearly thought otherwise.

> There were more <u>couples</u> in the <u>crowded</u> room than space <u>to dance</u>, but <u>in time</u> the furniture was removed. Jane wore a <u>flower</u> in her hair, <u>thus</u> signaling her desire to dance. She <u>may</u> regret this <u>last</u> decision, but not more than the one to ask Tom Lefroy <u>for</u> a lock of his hair. I am sure it will not be her last effort to shock, for she has many <u>years</u> ahead of her to wreak havoc upon my nerves.
>
> Jane must behave with discretion or her reputation will be ruined. Tom Lefroy may age like <u>a fine wine</u>, but at present he is a care-for-nothing flirt. He <u>must</u> mean her no harm, but at her <u>age</u> . . . If only sisters could be allowed the management of one another's hearts. This is not <u>to be</u> the first time I have persuaded her to favor the <u>sublime</u> over the ridiculous. <u>But</u> Jack Smith is not forgotten, for <u>first</u> love never is, though she never mentions him. Tom Lefroy is a distraction from the loss of Jack, but I warned her to be careful that he does not become more.
>
> <u>The</u> newest fashion in hats is for <u>grapes</u>, which <u>must</u> oblige us to <u>run</u> to the village for fresh trimmings for our hats. I am <u>quite</u> appalled at the quantity of fruit required, but Jane's plan for refurbishment of her straw bonnet is quite <u>clear</u> . . .

There was Cassandra's own sorrow, too, when we came to the passage about the death of her fiancé.

> *Jane is my comfort in these dark hours. She offers no advice, no recriminations against my dear Tom, only handkerchiefs and a glass of wine for my relief. My father feels the loss keenly, for now I am once more a burden he must discharge. But how shall I bring myself to think of marriage again? How could I forget my dearest Tom and accept a lesser man? For when set against his memory, they are all lesser men. Jane must be the one to marry, for I cannot.*

We learned from an entry written several years later that Jane's affection for the mysterious Jack Smith had fared no better than Cassandra's love for Tom Fowle.

> *Jane has written from London with unexpected news. Jack's ship went down off Portsmouth. She had written to renew her affection for him, much against my advice. I was right to persuade her to refuse his offer when it was made. What other advice could I have given? They would have had nothing to live on and no certainty for their future.*

So that was what had happened to the mysterious Jack Smith, the man Jane Austen had loved. He had died young, and Jane had been left to her regrets. I wondered if she had resented Cassandra for her well-meant, if somewhat tragic, advice. Would Jane rather have been poor and married than single with only the prospect of one day marrying someone wealthy?

"Wait a minute," Mimi said. "Turn back to where we started."

I did as she said. "What's the matter?"

She squinted at the faded writing. "Why are there words underlined in that part about Tom Lefroy?" Mimi pointed to a faint mark under one of the words. I fought back the impulse to snatch her finger away from the page. We ought to have been handling the diary with gloves on as it was.

"Careful." I contented myself with gently easing the diary out of her reach.

Cassandra Austen's handwriting, like most Georgian penmanship, held enough similarities to modern writing to make it readable, but it was quirky too. The *s*'s looked more like *f*'s, and some of the spellings were strange. But Mimi was right. Here and there, Cassandra had continued to underline random words. I flipped back to the beginning of the diary and leafed through the pages one by one.

I looked at Mimi. "Why would she do that?"

"Maybe it's some sort of a secret code?" Mimi said with mischief in her eyes. "So she could keep things from her nosy little sister."

I smiled at that, at the shared memory her words provoked. When I was twelve and Mimi was ten, I'd gone to extraordinary lengths to keep her from reading my diary, and she had gone to even more extraordinary lengths to thwart my efforts at secrecy.

"Mom always said they could have used you to help break the Enigma Code during World War II," I said, teasing her and enjoying it.

"You liked the challenge," she replied, flopping back on the bed pillows. "You loved to prove you were smarter than me."

"Prove? Prove?" I grabbed a pillow and tossed it at her. "My superior intelligence was self-evident. No proof necessary."

Mimi grasped the pillow and hugged it to her midsection. "I admit you're the smart one, except when it comes to being devious. You never were any good at that."

I should have continued to laugh, but her words caught me up short. If I had been a more devious person, I would have tried to undermine Daniel's relationship with Melissa all those years ago. I would have made a play for him, exploited his feelings for me. But I was my mother's daughter and, in a way, Jane Austen's too. Honor mattered more than anything, and stealing a man from another woman . . . well, it wasn't something an honorable woman, an Austen woman, would ever do.

"Ellen? Are you okay?" Mimi levered herself to a sitting position. "I didn't mean to offend you."

"What? Oh, I'm not offended. I just thought of something."

"What?"

I began flipping through the diary again. "The words . . . What if Cassandra didn't underline them as she went along?" I paused at a page where three random words had been heavily underscored. "Look. The ink where she drew the lines is darker than the words. Like it's newer, not as faded."

Mimi studied the page for a long moment. "We should make a list of the underlined words. From the beginning. In order." She took the diary from me. "If Cassandra went back afterward, maybe she really was trying to communicate with someone. A secret or something."

I reached for the pen and pad of hotel notepaper on the nightstand. "You call them out. I'll write them down."

"Okay. Ready?"

"Shoot."

Mimi flipped back to the first entry and began to scan the writing. "*Along. The. Narrow.*" She paused. "I think this one's underlined. *Way.*" She looked up at me. "*Along the narrow way?*"

Our eyes met, and I shivered despite the still summer warmth of the room.

"It *is* on purpose." I said the words so softly that I barely breathed them. A strange mixture of anxiety and excitement twisted in my stomach. We hadn't just been given a secret diary. We'd been given a diary with a secret.

"Keep reading," I commanded Mimi, who was only too happy to comply. She searched and I scribbled, and a few minutes later, we had this:

> *Along the narrow way it goes*
> *From house to house and back again*
> *A carpet for a traveler's woes*
> *That always brings one home again.*

I read it out loud, but once I had, the sparks of excitement I'd felt began to fizzle.

"That's it?" Mimi said, crestfallen. "It's just a riddle. And not even a very good one."

I shared her disappointment. "Mrs. Parrot said the Austen family liked riddles. Jane used them in *Emma*. It was probably just Cassandra's way of testing Jane to see if she was reading her diary. Nosy little sisters can't resist showing off when they figure something out."

Mimi sighed and closed the diary. "I'd argue with you, but it's true."

"So it's just a diary after all," I said.

"It's still Cassandra's diary," Mimi reminded me. "It's worth a fortune."

"No, it's an important literary artifact that will be donated to a museum." I could practically see the dollar signs in my sister's eyes.

Mimi wasn't to be persuaded. "If a museum wants it, they can buy it at auction."

"Mimi—"

"Mom gave it to us. She must have wanted us to benefit from it somehow. She knew I needed the money."

"How do you even know it belonged to Mom?" I hadn't wanted to put the thought into words, but with Mimi ready to hightail it for the nearest auction house, I had to offer some kind of reality check.

"You think she stole it?"

"I think we don't have any way of knowing. Not at the moment, anyway. We need time, Meems. Time to figure it all out." I paused. "You realize, don't you, that it's most likely a fake."

"No, it's real." Mimi crossed her arms and adopted that mulish expression that signaled her determination not to be persuaded. It seemed like a good time to change the subject.

"The riddle . . . What do you think it means?" I asked.

"How do you mean?"

"The riddle. There has to be an answer." I read it out loud again. "Probably a word or something. Jane used riddles in *Emma*, and they all led to a word."

Mimi shrugged. "Sounds like it's talking about a road or something."

"It's late. We're not going to solve this tonight. We should get some sleep. Start again in the morning." I picked up the diary and looked around for a new hiding place.

"I still think you should put it in the safe at the reception desk," Mimi said.

"I don't want anyone but you and me to know about this." I studied the room until I spotted the chintz skirt of the dressing table beneath the window. "Perfect." I rolled off the bed, reached over to lift the flowered material, and spied a drawer. "That will work."

"Not if someone really searches the room."

"The front desk will be closed by now, so I couldn't put it in the safe anyway. I'll leave a twenty-pound note on the nightstand. If anyone does come in looking for something to steal, I'll make it easy for them."

Mimi still looked uncomfortable, but she didn't object when I put the diary in the drawer and smoothed the fabric back down.

Mimi moved toward the door, but then paused with her hand on the knob. "Ellen?"

"Yes?"

She shook her head. "Nothing. See you in the morning."

"We can check for more riddles then. Let's meet extra early for breakfast."

"Okay." Mimi smiled and slipped out the door. "See you tomorrow."

Even if the riddles didn't amount to anything, they had at least given us a common objective. That was worth something.

I gave the dressing table one last pat and stood up. "Take care of that for us."

 went down early to breakfast and found Mimi already munching on granola and yogurt at the table in the bay window. We ate as quickly as we could and decided to meet in the garden to see if we could find any more riddles in the diary before the tour started for the day.

The early morning air smelled of damp, but in a fresh way. The birds sang in full chorus mode, and long rays of sun cut across the lawn. Mimi and I sat side by side on a bench as we went over the diary entries one by one.

Some had a lot of historical significance, such as the reference to Harris Bigg-Wither. My mother had told us of Jane's famous twenty-four-hour engagement. The death of the Reverend Mr. Austen had left Jane, her mother, and her sister in a bad financial situation, and sometime after Mr. Austen's death, when the sisters were in their mid- to late twenties, Jane had agreed to marry the younger brother of some friends. The young man had been wealthy but rather harsh and coarse, not a likely match for someone as clever as Jane, but Cassandra had clearly favored the match.

> *Harris Bigg-Wither will make a perfectly suitable husband. I have counseled Jane to act with prudence in this matter. He means to propose marriage, and she must accept him. I am not so far gone as to believe that happiness in marriage is entirely a matter of chance, but there is much to be said for practicality when a woman has passed the age of five and twenty. For myself, I could continue as we have been, although rented lodgings will never be my preference. But Jane . . . She needs time and a quiet corner to work upon her novels. True, a wife's duties might interfere, but what is the alternative?*

I stopped reading out loud at that point and looked at Mimi. "So Jane agreed to marry the guy because Cassandra talked her into it? That's a lot of sisterly influence."

Mimi frowned. "I think Cassandra was just being selfish. She knew if Jane snagged a rich guy, she'd be set."

I shook my head. "I'm sure she wanted what was best for her sister."

"Convenient that it would have been the best thing for her too."

"But Jane didn't marry the guy," I said, "since she changed her mind the next morning. I wonder what happened?"

"Keep reading," Mimi said. "I bet we're about to find out."
I took up the diary again.

> *Jane rebels against all sense. She came to my room past midnight and says she means to break the engagement at breakfast. Why can she not acknowledge the justice of this course? We quarreled as never before, and she fled my room before I could detain her. Foolish, headstrong girl. If Harris had offered for me, I would have accepted gladly in the knowledge that I could provide for my mother and sister. Jack Smith is gone, and Jane may never have another offer. The time has come to embrace practicality and give over any notion of romance.*
>
> *A gentleman learns to love once he has married, and from affection, devotion will follow . . .*

"So now we know," Mimi said. "Cassandra tried to push Jane into marriage, and she almost fell for it, but then she came to her senses."

"I don't think it's quite that simple." I scanned down to the next entry. "Listen."

> *Jane has taken out Elinor and Marianne and has begun to rework it. From what glimpses I can catch, it is an entirely new story. She was but eighteen when she wrote about the sisters, too early in her efforts to do them justice, but her anger at me over Mr. Bigg-Wither has lent fuel to the creative fire.*

"Look," Mimi said. "More underlining. It starts here." She pointed to the faint slash mark on the page.

I handed her the book. I decided I would much rather look for riddles than argue with her about whether Cassandra or Jane had been in the right in the Bigg-Wither affair. "Same as last night. You call them out, and I'll write them down."

We worked steadily for half an hour, aware that we only had a short time before the others would emerge from the hotel, ready to begin the day's tour. By the time we were done, we had three riddles.

We couldn't quite figure out the first one, although it didn't seem as if it should be that difficult.

> *A gentleman learns from an early age*
> *To play his part upon the stage*
> *His lines are crisp, his speech is clear*
> *He studies most from year to year.*

"What do you think?" Mimi looked at me. "Are we talking acting? Is this some Shakespeare reference that I don't get?"

I chuckled at that. "I don't think it means acting or the stage or anything like that."

"Why would an actor study from year to year, anyway?" Mimi sighed. "What's the point of these riddles? Other than Cassandra using them to psych out her little sister?"

"Maybe if we find all of them and figure out the answers, we'll know why she put them in here."

"I liked it better when all we had to do was choose a place to scatter Mom's ashes."

That was a sentiment we could share. "Me too."

"What's the next one? Read it out loud."

I bent over the hotel notepaper and did as instructed.

> *Couples crowd to dance in time*
> *A flower thus may last for years*
> *A wine must age to be sublime*
> *But first the grapes must run quite clear.*

I looked up from the paper, and Mimi was making a face. "Did it ever occur to you," she said, "that maybe Cassandra Austen is just weird? That maybe none of this means anything? I mean, what do couples and flowers and wine have to do with anything?"

"Well, I would think they had a good deal to do with the Austen sisters' lives. They were both on the lookout for a husband from what we've read so far. They would have been focused on clothes, parties, that sort of thing. That's why all these words are in her diary to begin with."

"Good point."

"Look, there's only one more."

"Plus the one we found last night."

I sighed. "C'mon, Meems. We're running out of time." I could hear the others on the opposite side of the hedge that shielded the garden from the drive.

Tailor, draper, seamstress all
Needles, thread and trimmings
Fashion, fair or rough or small
With trunks and boxes brimming

"That one should be right up my alley," Mimi said. "Since it has the word *fashion* in it."

"Maybe that's it. *Maybe fashion* is the solution."

We looked at each other in confusion. Mimi shook her head. "Even if we figure out what we think is the right answer, how do we ever know if we're correct?"

I folded up the notepaper and sighed. "I have no idea. It's probably just a wild-goose chase."

"Look, we've got the diary, right?" Mimi asked.

I nodded.

"Well, as long as we have the diary, the riddles don't matter that much. I mean, they might give it more value when we sell it—"

"Meems—"

"C'mon, Ellen. You know how much I need the money. You know what going out on my own means to me."

I did know, which was what worried me. I wondered if Mimi wanted to follow her dream so much that she would risk the career she'd built in the past fifteen years on a business venture that could never work. New businesses failed at an alarming rate, and frankly, I had no reason to believe that my sister's would be in the small percentage that were successful.

I looked at my watch, more to avoid this particular conversation than because I was worried about the time. "I'd better stash the diary in my room. Tom will fuss if we're late."

"We're going to have to figure this out at some point, Ell."

"I know. But not today. Besides, if we solve the riddles, it might make the diary even more valuable."

"True." Mimi sighed and stood up. "But—"

"We'll figure this out. Just not right now." I slipped the diary in my pack. "Save a spot for me in the van."

"Next to Daniel?" She grinned.

"Mimi—"

"I'll take that for a yes." She darted away toward the gap in the hedge.

I waved to the group when I crossed the drive to the hotel's entrance. "I forgot something in my room," I called to Tom. "Be right back."

I raced up the steps to my room and fumbled with the key on the old-fashioned lock. Then I stuffed the diary beneath the skirt of the dressing table. Not exactly Fort Knox, but it would do for the day. Maybe by the time the evening was over, we would solve the riddles and be one step closer to figuring out what to do with Cassandra Austen's diary.

CHAPTER SIXTEEN

llen walked with Daniel for the first part of the morning as we made our way through Chawton Woods, which I hoped was a good sign. It was pretty, of course, beneath the trees, the sunshine like polka dots over all the greenery, and the dust and leaves underfoot.

Ethan fell into step beside me as we started off. "I'm eager to see the diary you were talking about. Did you bring it?"

I shook my head. "I probably shouldn't have told you about it in the first place. My sister really wanted to keep it private."

"Cassandra Austen's diary?" he said. "Who would keep something like that a secret?"

"Shush!" I smiled to soften my scolding. "Like I said, Ellen doesn't think we should let anyone else know. I haven't told her yet that I mentioned it to you. I just don't think I can share it with you. Not unless she says it's okay."

Ethan pursed his lips. "I know we've only known each other a few days, but I thought . . . Never mind."

"Ethan—" But he didn't wait to hear my protest. With his much longer stride, he took off toward some of the others walking ahead of us.

I blinked back the tears that threatened. If I wanted to hook Ethan, I was going to have to figure out a way to sneak the diary away from Ellen so that he could see it. I didn't like the idea, but desperate times, even in Chawton Woods, called for desperate measures.

Still, there was nothing I could do until we returned to the hotel that afternoon. I tried to enjoy the walk through the sun-dappled woods, but my mind and heart were in too much turmoil.

After a while, we left the woods, walked along a road, and then cut up a gravel lane toward the train station at Medstead. We were supposed to take a short ride on a restored train line, but I hadn't given the actual experience much thought. I'd never ridden on a train before. I hoped it would turn out to be as romantic as it sounded.

The Watercress Line departed from a charmingly restored railway station. By then we'd been walking for a couple of hours. Mrs. Parrot met us at the station with the van, and we enjoyed our usual luscious snack. The water was flavored with elderflower cordial. As much as I'd resented having to go on this walking tour, I definitely enjoyed having all my needs catered to.

I followed Ethan onto the platform. He settled onto a bench in the shade, and I joined him, grateful to get out of the sun.

"Have you ridden this train before?" I asked. Maybe if I acted normal, we could get back on an even keel.

"I haven't been in the neighborhood that long."

He was only grumpy because of the heat, I assured myself, but I knew it wasn't true. He was taking my lack of trust in him very personally.

A rather tense silence descended. I didn't have the leisure of allowing things to unfold at a more natural pace. By noon on Friday, we'd all be headed our separate ways. The night before, lying in my bed and trying not to wilt from the heat, I'd thought about how Ethan was everything I'd ever wanted. Handsome. Rich. Successful. He treated me like a lady, or at least he did when he wasn't cranky.

"The station is charming, isn't it? There are air-raid posters in the old waiting room." On our way into the station, I'd ducked into the ladies' restroom, only to have to wait in line behind the others. So I'd had plenty of time to admire the scenery. "Keep calm and carry on. Stiff upper lip. All that sort of thing."

"I doubt they found it charming at the time."

Now he was just being childish.

"No, I doubt they did."

The whole diary thing was obviously bothering him. "There's the train." He stood up and moved to the edge of the platform. What else could I do but follow?

The train was from the 1830s, a bit after Jane Austen's time, but Cassandra would have lived to see how the railroad and its steam engines transformed the countryside. We all climbed aboard, and I decided I might as well go for broke, so I sat down on the hard leather seat next to Ethan. He did turn and smile at me briefly. Maybe he was just in a foul mood. Maybe whatever was bothering him didn't have anything to do with me or the diary.

And then he said the words that every woman hates to hear. "Mimi, if you don't feel you can trust me, then I don't see the point in pursuing this." He reached for my hand. "I haven't felt this way about a woman in a long time, but you must not feel the same way."

"But I do."

"Then let me help you. Let me into your life."

What was I supposed to do? I couldn't betray Ellen any more than I already had. The train rumbled onward as I hesitated, and the conductor came down the aisle dressed in period attire with a long coat, vest, cravat, and brass buttons.

"Tickets, please."

Tom waved him over and took care of our fares, but I had a feeling that he was keeping one eye on me as well.

"You gave the impression that you were interested in a serious relationship," Ethan said, "but I don't think that's the case."

The train lurched, and so did my stomach. A part of me wanted to confront him, because how was I supposed to know whether he was really interested in me or just the diary, the way he kept going on about it? But I was too exhausted, too confused, and my feet hurt too much to fight anymore. Not to mention that my pride had taken a serious blow. "I wasn't aware I'd given you any impression at all." I smiled and tossed my hair a little bit. "I mean, I'm enjoying your company, Ethan, but . . . well, isn't that what we're supposed to do on a walking tour? Make new friends?" I put plenty of emphasis on the last word.

His face darkened. "Yes. Yes, we are. And I'm glad we're friends, for the record." Although he certainly didn't sound like it. "How are your feet?" Now he could afford to be concerned. Now that he'd shown me how unconcerned he actually was.

"They're fine." They burned like fire, of course, but since I had decided on Sunday night that I would walk through hot coals to win over a man like Ethan, I could hardly complain.

We sat for the remaining twenty minutes of the train ride in relative silence. Ethan kept his gaze focused out the window, and I kept mine away from him. A low murmur from the others behind me told me that the awkward, stiff conversation and our current silence had not gone unnoticed.

I was very grateful when the train finally pulled into the station at Alresford. I leaped for the door, and another costumed conductor waited outside to help me down. Tom ushered everyone through the station—just as charmingly restored as the one at Medstead—and out into the plaza in front.

Once again, Mrs. Parrot was there with the van. I looked at it longingly. I could ride in pain-free comfort to the pub where we were scheduled to eat lunch. But then I made the mistake of glancing at Ethan. He had turned his charm on the gaggle of Austenites, and even the two married women were leaning in his direction. His magnetism was universal, it seemed.

I should have known better. I did know better. Ten years ago I would have pegged him for what he was right away. But ten years ago I wasn't thirty-six and still single. Ten years ago I'd never even contemplated Botox or a brow lift. Ten years ago the world had been my oyster, and I had been its pearl.

Jane and Cassandra Austen had never planned to be spinsters either. Cassandra had been engaged. Jane had been a flirt. Even with almost no money, they'd expected to marry one day. What if I turned out to be like the Austen sisters? Honestly, I'd never considered the possibility that I might end up permanently single.

Ellen stood a little apart from the group, taking pictures of the sign for the Watercress Line and the bright flowers that surrounded the station. I'd always suspected Ellen would never marry. I knew she'd given her heart long ago to Daniel. But now here he was, clearly trying to win her back, and she was barely giving him a chance, while I had just struck out with perhaps the most eligible man I'd ever met. Our roles were well and truly reversed.

I didn't like that realization very much either.

❧❧❧❧❧

When we set off from Alresford, Ethan wasn't with us. I hadn't seen him leave, but Tom said he'd gotten an urgent phone call and caught a taxi home. I didn't believe it for a minute, of course. He was unhappy with me, and he was letting me know.

Tom herded us away from the station and along a steep path until we reached a road. Thankfully, this one had a wide sidewalk, and when it took a climb uphill, I dropped back, eager to be alone. I wasn't going to be allowed much solitude though. I could see Tom up ahead, talking intently to Ellen, gesturing and nodding down the road, and then he stood there as the group passed. He waited patiently while I climbed the hill with all the enthusiasm of a snail.

"I can call Mrs. Parrot to bring the van," he said, with no attempt to be subtle.

His words were the straw that broke the camel's back. I burst into tears and turned away, leaning against the brick wall that separated the front garden of the houses from the pavement.

"Mimi? What's wrong?"

"Nothing. I'm fine. Just a little . . . stressed." Sweat poured from every possible outlet on my body. My feet ached, and I could feel the beginnings of a sunburn on my cheeks and nose. No wonder Ethan had fled.

"You're not fine." A handkerchief appeared in my line of vision. "Do you have any water left?"

"Yes." I took the handkerchief, wiped my eyes, and then slid my daypack off my shoulders. I reached for the water bottle without looking at Tom. While getting dumped by Ethan was embarrassing, being tended to by a man whom I'd rejected was even more humbling.

"Thanks." I tried to hand Tom his handkerchief. At first he waved it away, but then he changed his mind and reached for it. He also took my water bottle from my hand, poured some of the contents on the handkerchief, and when it was good and wet, draped the cloth around my neck.

Bliss. Instant, incredible bliss.

"That feels . . . " I couldn't even think of the word.

"We don't want any of our hikers to get heatstroke."

If I'd expected any sympathy, I wasn't getting it. "Oh no. Of course not. I'm slowing down the group enough as it is."

He wasn't being kind. Just professional. A flush rose in my cheeks, but I was already so red in the face that it wouldn't even show. Maybe the heat had some useful purpose after all.

"Mimi—"

I waved him toward the road where the others were disappearing over the top of the hill. "I'm okay. Go on and tend to the group."

"I can't leave you here alone."

"I'll catch up." But we both knew that was doubtful.

He reached into his pocket for his cell phone. "I'm calling Mrs. Parrot."

"No. No, you're not."

Determination welled up inside of me. I had no idea where it came from. I was and always had been a girlie girl, perfectly happy to be rescued by a variety of charming princes on any and every occasion. But this time was different. I was tired of waiting for men to do the right thing. This time I was going to rescue myself.

I pulled the handkerchief from my neck. "Here." I thrust it back at Tom. "Let's go." I grabbed my pack and took off up the hill.

Every step was agony. My feet, my aching muscles, the sweat that beaded my forehead and rolled down my spine. I couldn't remember ever being in that much physical misery. I wasn't going to quit though. I would show Ethan. I'd show Ellen and Tom too, for that matter. I was more than just an accessory.

I might not be able to pull anyone else's weight, but I could sure as shooting pull my own.

CHAPTER SEVENTEEN

fter the pub lunch that I was coming to know and love, I opted out of the afternoon walk along the river. It was the perfect excuse to spend more time deciphering the riddles in Cassandra's diary. Mimi was determined to keep walking, and she seemed so fragile after Ethan disappeared that I didn't push her to return to the hotel with me. I ignored the pitying looks the others sent her way. It had been a long time since I'd had to witness one of her romantic dramas firsthand. That was the beauty of living three states apart. But to see her like this, to watch her scheme to catch Ethan unravel in front of God and everybody—it was more painful than I could have ever imagined.

I tried to turn my thoughts to something else. I tried to focus on the novel experience of being driven on what was, to me, the wrong side of the road. I tried to pay attention to the wind blowing through the open passenger window of the van, the cottages clustered here and there so close to the edge of the road that it was a wonder we didn't sideswipe any of them. Mrs. Parrot drove the van as if she were Admiral Nelson bent on conquering the French navy at the Battle of Trafalgar. I was sure she would settle for nothing less than total domination of the British roads.

The heat had abated somewhat by the time we arrived at the hotel. I took a shower and sat on the bed, thinking about Cassandra's diary. The chintz skirt of the dressing table still provided protective cover to my secret. I leaned over, lifted the skirt, and reached for the diary.

It wasn't there.

I whirled around. The twenty-pound note was still on the bedside table. Nothing else appeared to have been touched. Just the diary.

I flicked back the chintz again, my heart in my throat, but the diary definitely wasn't there.

A random thief wouldn't have taken the time to find such an obscure and, on the surface, worthless object. He or she would have grabbed the money on my bedside table and made a dash for it.

I sank down on the bed.

The diary was gone.

Mrs. Parrot hadn't been with us that morning. No, she'd only met up with us at the pub for lunch. She could have looted the entire hotel with all the time she'd had.

Then I remembered that I hadn't been the last one at the van that morning. Daniel had come out of the hotel behind me.

No, it had to be Mrs. Parrot. Of course it was her. Hadn't I suspected from the beginning that she knew about the diary?

Anger lodged in my throat, a thick knot that burned. I could hardly confront her. She'd deny everything, and I would look like an idiot. Or a crazy person. I needed Mimi. For the first time in years, I felt a desperate longing for my sister. Well, that wasn't strictly true. I had felt that longing fairly recently. Every time I'd driven my mother to the hospital for her chemotherapy. Oh, I'd disguised my need for her as anger. Anger that she couldn't be bothered to fly in from Atlanta and shoulder her share of the burden. But what I'd really needed every time I'd made that drive from my mother's house to the hospital was my sister.

I didn't know if Mrs. Parrot wanted the diary for its monetary value or merely for its own sake. I suspected she wanted it simply for the thrill of possessing it, given her devotion to Jane Austen. If that was the case, I thought, rising from the bed in sudden agitation, then it might still be somewhere in the hotel. Most likely in her room.

How was I going to get into her room though? I happened to know which one it was because she'd been in line in front of me when we checked in the night before. Her room was on the floor above mine, but at the back of the hotel. It would be locked, of course, and besides, she had driven me back to Langrish Hall. She was probably in there right now.

I heard the crunch of footsteps on the gravel drive outside my window. When I looked outside, I spied the familiar tweed jacket and Day-Glo orange hair heading toward a walking trail at the side of the hotel.

Perhaps my luck wasn't completely disastrous.

I tiptoed from the room—at least my version of tiptoeing—and made my way upstairs. As it turned out, it wasn't locked. It was, however, occupied by the maid, who was cleaning.

"I'll just be a moment," she said with a smile and a glance at the old-fashioned room key I had clutched in my hand. "If you don't mind."

"Oh no. No trouble." I wasn't about to correct her mistaken assumption that I was the occupant of the room. "I'll just wait out here."

It was a dangerous game, I knew, because Mrs. Parrot could return at any moment, but I wasn't looking to steal anything. Just the opposite. I was only interested in getting back what belonged to me.

Thankfully, the young woman finished almost immediately. She moved away with her small cart, and I slipped inside and closed the door behind me.

I didn't know it was possible to shake quite so much. My hands trembled as I pulled open drawers, lifted bed pillows, and explored under the mattress. The bathroom offered no concealment whatsoever. I stood in the middle of the room and slowly surveyed its contents. Really, there was no other place to hide something like the diary, except . . .

I disliked doing it, but I reached for Mrs. Parrot's suitcase. It looked like one that would have belonged to my mother, an ancient piece of hard-sided luggage that could probably withstand nuclear winter. I picked it up off the floor, set it on the bed, and pulled at the latches.

Nothing happened. It was obviously locked. The old-fashioned way, with a key that no doubt hung at this very moment around Mrs. Parrot's neck.

I noticed how heavy the suitcase was when I returned it to its place on the floor beside the bed. From the weight of it and the dull thuds it made, I guessed that it was full of books. Definitely more than one. But whether it contained Cassandra's diary . . . well, that was only conjecture on my part.

I was ready to flee the scene of my near-crime when the door opened, and Mrs. Parrot stood there in the doorway.

"Pardon?" She looked as flustered as I felt.

"I'm sorry. I—" What? What could I possibly say? "I mean, I came to see you, and the maid was here, cleaning. She said I should just wait for you in here." I resisted the urge to cross my fingers behind my back. That would have been childish. As if worming my way into someone's hotel room under false pretenses wasn't.

"How extraordinary." Mrs. Parrot came into the room and shut the door behind her. Obviously she didn't believe me.

"I know. Isn't it?" I decided to play dumb. "Your room has a much better view than mine." I nodded toward the window. "Plus, you don't have to listen to people and cars crunching across the gravel at all hours of the day and night."

"If it's a problem, I could see about a different—"

"Oh no. It's fine."

A long moment of silence reigned. Finally, Mrs. Parrot cleared her throat. "You said you wanted to speak to me?"

"Oh, um, yes. That is . . . " What on earth was I going to say? "It's, um, well, it's about the Austens again."

"What about the Austens?"

"I was asking you about them the other day, and I just wondered . . . that is . . . my mother mentioned something once called *Elinor and Marianne*. Is that a lost Jane Austen novel or something?"

Mrs. Parrot frowned. "Actually, that was the first version of *Sense and Sensibility*. It was originally a novel in letters."

"I've never seen it in a bookstore."

"No, well, you wouldn't, because there are no existing manuscripts. She wrote it first as a teenager, but later, after the Austen ladies settled at Chawton, she revised it into the novel that we know."

"Oh." And because of the diary, I knew why she had gone back to rework that particular story.

"Is that all you wanted to know?"

"What? Oh, um, yes. Thank you." I edged toward the door. "Sorry to have disturbed you. And sorry about . . . " I looked around at the room. "Sorry about being in here. Really, if the maid hadn't insisted . . . " Poor girl. But I doubted Mrs. Parrot would pursue the matter, because I was pretty sure she didn't believe me.

"I shall see you at dinner then."

"Yes. I'll see you then."

I couldn't have seemed any guiltier if I'd confessed on the spot. I scurried from the room in shame and frustration. If Mrs. Parrot did have the diary, we were never going to get it back. She would make sure of that.

CHAPTER
EIGHTEEN

llen and Daniel looked very happy sitting together at dinner, and I tried to give them some space. My sister kept darting nervous glances at me, and I knew that she was worried that her happiness might be difficult for me to handle in light of Ethan's defection. No one had seen him since he'd disappeared in the taxi after the train ride.

After dinner I wandered into the garden in front of the hotel with my copy of *Sense and Sensibility*. Now that I knew how closely the book was connected to the actual experience of the Austen sisters, I'd begun to find it more interesting. I'd been reading the book in odd spare moments and had, both to my delight and embarrassment, quickly become engrossed. Elinor and Marianne Dashwood's similarity to Ellen and me was just short of eerie, but what intrigued me more was the similarity between the Austen sisters and the fictional Dashwood girls. Were all sisters the same?

Enough daylight lingered in the English summer that I could get another chapter of the book in before darkness fell. If you discounted the occasional power line or cell tower in the dusky, surrounding hills, you could imagine that the house and the scenery looked very much like it might have in Jane Austen's time. In the quiet countryside, past and present blurred, and that wasn't necessarily a bad thing.

Part of me longed to go to Ellen's room, curl up on her bed, and have her tell me that everything was going to be okay. That had been our pattern for years. Or at least it had been our pattern until I moved to Atlanta. I thought of our house in Dallas, where Ellen still lived. I'd only ever seen it through jaded eyes. Too small, too plain, too ordinary. But after the day's events, I almost longed for its shelter and for the simplicity of the life I'd had when I lived there.

I wondered if Jane Austen had felt that way, too, about her father's rectory at Steventon. Tom had told us she was never happy when she lived in Bath, and that it was only after several years of moving from place to place, when she, Cassandra, and their mother moved to the cottage at Chawton, that she found contentment again.

I'd had that contentment in our little house in Dallas with my mother and my sister, only I'd been too young and foolish to realize it.

I settled onto a wooden bench tucked into a corner of the garden. Whoever had cornered the market on these benches must have made a fortune. Everywhere you turned in England, there was a strategically placed bench like this. Usually they said something like "For Ethel, who loved this garden." They gave you such a sense of place, those plaques. That was what I lacked, I realized. A sense of place. Of belonging.

Footsteps crunched across the gravel on the other side of the hedge that separated my bench from a direct view of the hotel. I hoped it was someone headed to the parking lot and not into the little sanctuary I'd found.

"Mimi?"

It was Tom. I bit back a sigh of exasperation. I wasn't sure I was strong enough to bear being comforted at the moment.

"Over here." I could tell him, politely of course, that I wanted to be alone, and he would make himself scarce, but even I had a hard time being that rude.

"Am I intruding?" I appreciated that he asked. Ethan, who should have been more courtly by nature and nurture, would simply have assumed it was his right to join me.

That thought didn't make his defection any easier to bear.

"It's okay." I gestured to the bench beside me. "I'm just enjoying the evening."

"Much better now that the sun's gone down." He sat beside me. Not too close, but not at the other end of the bench either. "I don't mean to bother you, but you were in rough shape this afternoon."

"Yes. I was." To my exasperation, tears stung my eyes. Again. I was tired of springing a leak every time I turned around. "I'm okay though. Thanks for checking."

"I don't think you are okay." Tom placed an arm along the back of the bench so that his hand was near, but not touching, my shoulder. He didn't look at me though. Instead, he gazed out into the dusk. "You can admit it."

"Easy for you to say."

He chuckled, and we sat in silence for a long time. Tom Braddock was comfortable company, I'd give him that. With most men, I would feel the need to charm or entertain them. With Tom, I could just . . . be.

"Are you happy with how the tour's going?" I asked him. Time to move the focus away from my man troubles. "I know you said it was your first time doing this walk."

"We've hit a few snags, but on the whole, I'm pleased."

"It's too bad that whoever thought up the tour couldn't participate. They must have been pretty special to get to choose everything."

"I believe she was special," Tom said softly. "The owner of the tour company went to school with her."

"But you had to find all the daily routes. Figure out where to house us all, feed us."

"It's not that much different from the Air Force." He stretched out his legs and crossed them at the ankles. "Except that I can't yell at the recruits."

"I doubt you had to do much yelling." While he was not an intimidating man, he was definitely an authoritative one.

"No." Even in the dusk I could see his smile. It was a nice smile. "Not much."

I had the sudden urge to slide closer to him on the bench. To lean against him and let my head rest against his shoulder. The feeling startled me, and it brought back the memory of his kiss the day before. I forced myself to stay right where I was.

"Do you miss it?" I asked. "The service?"

"I miss the camaraderie, but, no, I don't miss that way of life. I was ready to settle down." His shoulders tensed. "I should have done that sooner."

He was referring to his late wife, of course. "It's hard to know, though, isn't it, when it's time to move on? To do something different?" I'd felt that way myself almost every day for the past three years. My dream of owning my own store was within reach, but not without a hefty amount of risk. I hadn't had the courage to gamble everything I had on my dream. At least, not yet.

"What about you?" Tom asked. "Are you happy in the life you're leading?"

He might as well have been reading my mind. "Yes. And no."

"Ah."

"What does that mean? *Ah*?"

"Just *ah*." I could hear the smile in his voice. Darkness had fallen, and I could no longer make out his expression. The anonymity of the night made confession all that much easier.

"I want to go into business for myself," I said.

"What kind of business?"

"A clothing store. A boutique. Something trendy but not too edgy."

"In Atlanta?"

"I was thinking about going back home to Dallas."

Wait a minute! What was I saying? Hadn't I been thinking about New York every spare moment?

"Why Dallas?"

His question surprised me. "Well, I guess because it's my home."

"When we first met and I asked you about Texas, you didn't sound very enthusiastic."

I thought about it for a moment. "I guess if I'm going to put down roots somewhere, it might as well be a place that feels familiar."

"Would you ever consider living anywhere else?"

"I guess it depends."

"On what?"

"What the other place had to offer."

"Yes. I guess it would."

I thought he might make a move then, but he stayed where he was, still relaxed, still a comforting presence. My eyelids grew heavy, and my body felt so languid. I didn't know if it was all the walking, the heavy meal, or the company. My eyes must have drifted closed, because the next thing I knew, I felt Tom's hand on my shoulder.

"Mimi?"

"*Hmm?*"

"I think we'd better get you inside. Otherwise they'll find you here in the morning, sound asleep on the lawn."

"You say that like it's a bad thing."

He laughed then, and the sound of it warmed me. "Come on." He took my hand in the dark and tugged me off the bench. We started toward the hotel, and to my surprise, he kept my hand in his. His grip was warm and firm without being controlling. We crunched across the driveway, and he opened the door for me. At the foot of the stairs, he squeezed my hand.

"I'll see you in the morning."

"What time is breakfast?"

"They start serving at seven. Do you need a wake-up call?"

"No." Now that we were inside under the glare of electric lights, I didn't feel quite so comfortable with him. I pulled my hand from his. "I have a travel alarm."

"Okay then. Good night."

He turned toward the hallway a few steps away, and I watched him go with regret. I was surprised he hadn't walked me to my door, but maybe I had misinterpreted his interest. Maybe he was just being a good tour leader by following me into the garden. A few days ago, I would have wanted that to be the case. Now, though, as I made my way wearily up the stairs, I felt quite differently about Tom Braddock.

Which was a bigger discovery, in a way, than the riddles in Cassandra's diary—and just as puzzling.

t dinner the night before, Mimi
and I had agreed to meet very early
for breakfast to try to finish solving
the riddles. I had left the windows
open in my room to relieve some of the heat, so the birdsong at
first light woke me bright and early. I sat up in bed and picked
up the list of riddles from the nightstand.

"What are you trying to tell us?" I was reduced to talking
to an inanimate object.

I took a quick shower and headed downstairs, but Mimi was
already there, seated at the table in the bay window.

"This is a first," I said, nodding at her with approval. The
night before, I hadn't been able to bring myself to tell her that
the diary was missing. I was going to have to confess sooner or
later. Probably sooner, and then I would have to admit that I
should have listened to her suggestion about the hotel safe.

She stuck out her tongue at me and then smiled. "Don't be so bossy, or I won't help you with the riddles."

"Can I be bossy enough to help myself to some of your coffee?" I nodded toward the French press on the table.

"All right. But you owe me."

The easy camaraderie was as welcome as it was unexpected.

"So did you have any blinding insights in the middle of the night?" I asked her. "Any symbolic dreams that would simplify this whole thing?"

Mimi sighed. "I wish. What about you?"

I poured my coffee and stirred in a lump of sugar. "Let's get to work." I pulled the sheet of paper containing the transcribed riddles from my pocket. Mimi took it from me, unfolded it, and laid it on the table. She reread the first one.

Along the narrow way it goes
From house to house and back again
A carpet for a traveler's woes
That always brings one home again.

"So what's *it?*" I asked her. "*Along the narrow way it goes?*"

"*From house to house?*" She fiddled with the handle of her coffee cup. "A salesman, maybe?" she said with a smile.

"I'm pretty sure they'd never heard of the Fuller Brush guy back then." I laughed. "Really, what's narrow, goes from house to house, and has something to do with travelers?"

Mimi smiled. "That's easy. It's a road."

"Good." I let out a little sigh of relief. Maybe this part wouldn't be that hard after all. "What about the next one?" I picked up the paper from the table to read.

> *A gentleman learns from an early age*
> *To play his part upon the stage*
> *His lines are crisp, his speech is clear*
> *He studies most from year to year.*

"That doesn't even make sense." Mimi frowned. "Is she talking about a theater or something?"

I took another sip of coffee. "Or it could mean 'school,' or something like that. *Learns* and *studies*. Maybe Cassandra meant where a gentleman gets his education."

"Okay, then we've got *road* and *school*. What's next?"

I read the third riddle again.

> *Couples crowd to dance in time*
> *A flower thus may last for years*
> *A wine must age to be sublime*
> *But first the grapes must run quite clear.*

"No clue," Mimi said.

"Wait." Excitement rose in my chest, because I was starting to get a feel for Cassandra Austen's turn of mind. "What do the three things have in common?"

Mimi scanned the paper again. "Well, I just read in *Sense and Sensibility* about a ball with too many people to fit in the room being called a *squeeze*. And that's what you do to grapes to get wine."

"But not to a flower to make it last," I said. "That you have to *press*."

We sat in silence for a moment, sipping our coffee.

"Let's move on to the last one," Mimi said. She read it out loud.

> *Tailor, draper, seamstress all*
> *Needles, thread and trimmings*
> *Fashion, fair or rough or small*
> *With trunks and boxes brimming*

"I've been thinking about that one." Mimi tossed the paper to the table. "It's clothes, of course." She leaned back in her chair. "It doesn't make sense, though, when you put them together. *Road*, *clothes*, *school* and *press*. What do those things have in common? Maybe we don't have the words right."

"What do you mean?" I asked.

"Well, that first one," Mimi said. "It could mean *road* or *street* or even *highway*."

"*Clothes squeeze*," I read. "But that doesn't make any sense. The closest thing I can think of would be a pants press."

"Pants press?" Mimi looked at me incredulously. "Like that thing in our hotel room in London?" The strange contraption—strange to us Americans, at least, who made do with an iron and ironing board—was a staple in British hotels.

"That doesn't make sense, though, does it?" I studied the list of words again. What if we'd gotten the riddle wrong? We might have mistaken a stray mark for underlining. And now we didn't have the diary to be sure.

"Besides," Mimi said with a small laugh, "I think *pants* means underwear over here. Isn't it called a trouser press?"

"We'll never figure this out." I wasn't usually so pessimistic, but with the prospect of confessing the loss of the diary looming over me, I wasn't feeling very positive. I had to tell Mimi the truth about the theft. "Look, Meems, I should have come to your room last night and talked to you."

Her face scrunched up in a funny expression. "It's okay, Ell. I don't need sympathy."

"What?"

"I know I made a fool of myself with Ethan. I probably got what I deserved."

I hated that for her, but at least she was taking some responsibility for a change.

"I'm sorry." And I was. However strained our relationship might have been, I wanted my sister to be happy.

"Thanks."

"But that's not what I meant about coming to talk with you." I took a deep breath. "I guess I have a confession of my own to make."

She leaned back in her chair and smiled. "This should be good. Is it Daniel? Have you two gotten together?"

"No. I mean, maybe. I don't know. But that's not what I should have talked to you about." *Oh dear.*

"What is it?" she said, exasperated. "C'mon, Ell. It can't be that bad."

"It's the diary."

Her face fell, and so did my stomach.

"It's gone, isn't it?" She didn't ask it as a question. In fact, it was almost as if she was expecting it.

"When I got back early yesterday afternoon, it wasn't there. Someone's taken it."

Mimi's face went white as a sheet.

At that moment, our tête-à-tête was interrupted by none other than Mrs. Parrot. She came into the small dining room carrying a glass of orange juice from the cold buffet outside the door. The color of the juice matched her hair.

"Good morning, Ellen. Mimi. Would you mind if I joined you?" She didn't wait for an answer before pulling out a chair at our table.

"Please do," I said, although I didn't really mean it. I folded the notepaper and slipped it into my pocket. Mimi shot me a frustrated look. Then she sent Mrs. Parrot a more malevolent one.

"How are you both feeling this morning?" Mrs. Parrot looked at us through the thick lenses of her glasses, as if examining two bugs under a microscope.

"We're very well, thank you," Mimi said in her most prim and proper voice. "And you?"

"Also very well, thank you."

Silence fell, and a waiter appeared. Mrs. Parrot ordered a pot of tea and brown toast.

"Are you looking forward to Selborne today?" she asked.

"I'm sure it will be lovely," I said. How was I supposed to carry on as if this were a normal piece of breakfast chitchat? "Is there anything in particular we should look for on the walk?" It was hard to think about anything but Cassandra's diary and her riddles, especially when my main suspect for the diary theft was happily buttering her toast in front of me.

"Anything special? No, no." Mrs. Parrot poured out her tea. "Simply enjoy the beauty."

Mimi's gaze shot daggers at Mrs. Parrot, but I sent her a warning look. No way was I going to let her attack the woman without proof. Not after the awkward scene when Mrs. Parrot found me lurking in her room, and not when I couldn't be one hundred percent sure that this woman was the culprit. That was another thing Mimi didn't know about. She still didn't know that Daniel knew about the diary.

Mimi sat down her coffee cup and looked at the older woman. "Mrs. Parrot, there's something I've been meaning to ask you."

Uh-oh. I could see where this was going. Mimi's style could be considered confrontational under the best of circumstances.

I leaped into the fray. "Will you be walking into Selborne with us today?"

"No, no, my dear. I'm afraid it's a bit too rough for me."

"Oh." What else was I supposed to say?

"Mrs. Parrot—" Mimi was not to be dissuaded.

I jumped in again. "We've enjoyed seeing you this morning, but Mimi and I really need to run back to our rooms and finish packing."

"Of course, dears. Needs must." She smiled at us quite fondly, really, which seemed strange.

I practically dragged Mimi out of her chair. "C'mon, sis. We don't have much time."

Mimi's arm was rigid beneath my hand, but she cooperated, thank goodness. I knew I'd pay for my intervention later though.

I led her from the breakfast room, away from Mrs. Parrot and the potential explosion of accusations.

"You should have let me confront her," Mimi hissed as we moved toward the stairs. "What if she took the diary?"

"She wouldn't have admitted anything." I shoved her up the staircase in front of me.

"Maybe not," she said over her shoulder, "but she would have given herself away somehow. We've got to get that diary back."

"We will, okay? But we can't just accuse someone of theft without proof."

"Then we'll get proof."

I sighed and climbed the stairs after her. "I certainly hope so, Meems. I certainly hope so."

CHAPTER TWENTY

y sister should have let me confront Mrs. Parrot. She had to have been the one who took the diary, because if she wasn't . . . Well, she had to have taken it.

Ellen hustled me off to my room and told me to leave finding the diary to her. I didn't want to agree, but she looked so distressed—and I felt so guilty—that I finally gave in.

Thursday was our last full day of walking. I emerged from the hotel a little early so that I could get Tom to help me with my feet.

"I'll be glad to," he said when I asked him for a little blister triage. He led me back into the garden and the bench where we'd sat the night before. His offer of assistance and the reminder of our nighttime confidences made me uncomfortable, but not in an uneasy way. It was more that I'd let him come too close, and now I wasn't sure how to put distance between us again.

Somehow having another person tend to my feet, especially a male person, felt exceptionally intimate. Tom probably did this all the time in his role as tour leader, but I couldn't remember the last time someone had performed first aid on me like that. Actually, I could. My mother couldn't stand the sight of blood, so it was usually my sister who wound up having to squirt the Bactine on my injuries and apply the Band-Aids.

Tom eyed his handiwork. "It looks like everything is holding up pretty well."

"I guess so." I sighed. "Are you sure you can't just magically heal them?"

He finished applying the last blister patch and patted the top of my foot. "I would if I could." Then he winked at me.

I would never have figured Tom Braddock for a winking kind of guy, but he did have amazing silver-blue eyes. The wink emphasized the lines around the corner of his eyes.

Soon the others joined us, and Tom gave his now-traditional beginning-of-the-day introduction.

"The village we're visiting today, Selborne, was the home of Gilbert White," he began. "He was a famous eighteenth-century naturalist. It's almost certain that he was acquainted with Jane Austen's father, as they were both clergymen and lived within a few miles of one another."

To my relief, Ethan didn't appear that morning. I overheard one of the Austenites ask Tom about him, but Tom's answer was noncommittal. "He may catch up with us at Selborne" was all he had said. I was relieved by Ethan's absence but also worried.

What if he, and not Mrs. Parrot, had taken the diary? How in the world would I ever get it back?

There was nothing I could do at the moment, so I focused on putting one foot in front of the other as we made our way toward Selborne. The walk into the village skirted fields and rambled down country lanes overhung with leafy tree limbs. We climbed our first hanger, or hill, as we made our way through Selborne Common, a wooded area with occasional open spaces. We mounted a ridge, crested the hill, and then descended once more into the valley. Underfoot, the ground was slippery with dried leaves. For all that I had dreaded coming to England, I had, despite my blisters, found a measure of peace in walking the footpaths and byways.

As we drew closer to the village, we began to pass the most darling little cottages, all thatched roofs and climbing roses, and the sight of them lifted my spirits. Each one seemed to contain a breathtakingly beautiful front garden, and before we even reached the village, I was in love. How could anyone who ever visited this place contemplate leaving?

We came to the edge of the village green, which Tom informed us in Hampshire was called a plestor. Mrs. Parrot was waiting once again with the van and the refreshments, and I gratefully claimed a large glass of orange-flavored water. The day had grown more humid so that by midmorning my T-shirt clung to me. If it hadn't been for the nettles, I would have zipped off the lower part of my convertible hiking pants. My fear of nettles, though, won out over my need for comfort.

"We'll rest a few minutes here, then set off down the lythe," Tom said. *Lythe* was another Hampshire term—it meant "valley."

We passed the church and then came to the edge of the churchyard. From there, we had a beautiful view down the length of the valley.

"This is the Short Lythe," Tom said. "Beyond it is the Long Lythe. We'll walk to the end and then circle back through the trees over there. That will lead us back into the village and to—"

"A pub for lunch," we all chorused, now accustomed to the routine.

Mrs. Parrot took our lunch orders and refilled our water bottles, and then we set off.

For the first time, I walked in the front of the group with Tom. It was much less stressful now, not having to position myself so that I could "accidentally" end up next to Ethan. Tom and I chatted as we made our way down the steep descent into the valley, and I felt more peaceful than I had in a long time. I enjoyed walking with him at the front.

"How are the feet holding up?" Tom asked as we made our way under a canopy of tree limbs.

"Don't fuss." I smiled at him to show that I appreciated his concern, but his shoulders stiffened.

"I wasn't fussing." He'd been smiling a moment ago, but now he was looking straight ahead. Great. I'd allowed myself to forget for a moment that Tom was, in fact, a guy. And guys never liked to be scolded, especially if they were showing concern.

"I'm sorry. I appreciate your helping me. A lot. Otherwise I'd be stuck back in the van with Mrs. Parrot."

"What's wrong with Mrs. Parrot?"

Now I'd really put my foot in it. "Nothing. Sorry. I'm just—"

"We're fortunate to have someone of her caliber on this trip."

"Yes. Of course we are." Tears stung my eyes. I'd alienated the one ally I had left.

"It's a shame Ethan couldn't make it." He didn't even look at me as he spoke.

"No, it isn't."

"Are you sure?"

Now he was making me mad. "I realize I've been an idiot, okay? No need to rub it in."

Tom cast a glance over his shoulder, and I did the same. The others had dropped back so that we were virtually alone.

"Ethan said he had to go back to London on urgent business." He paused. "I didn't want to say anything before . . . I thought you would think it was sour grapes. But Ethan has a reputation."

"He's a womanizer, you mean."

"That, but there's more."

How much more could there be?

"Ethan inherited the house at Deane from his mother."

"He told me that."

"Did he tell you that it's falling down around his ears? And that he doesn't have the money to keep it up, much less renovate it?"

"I thought he was a banker in the city, or something like that."

Tom shook his head. "No."

A jolt of realization shook me. "Ethan thought I had money when we first met. Didn't he?" And not just a little money. Cassandra's-diary-at-auction kind of money.

"I think he thought you were a woman of means."

"And he thought he would find a wealthy Austenite who would love the chance to date someone related to Jane Austen. Why didn't you warn me?" Anger flared in my chest. "You could have said something sooner."

Tom looked at me as we walked and arched one eyebrow. "Would you have believed me?"

We both knew the answer.

"Sometimes," Tom said, "we have to learn a lesson for ourselves."

What he said should have sounded paternalistic and condescending, but instead it just sounded like the truth. My cheeks flushed with embarrassment, and I prayed for the sudden appearance of a sinkhole in the middle of the Long Lythe.

When none appeared, I stepped to the side of the path and bent down to tie my shoe, although it was already firmly tied. Thankfully, Tom kept walking, and I saw Ellen move up beside him to take my place.

I trailed behind them for the rest of the hike. Soon enough, the two of them were smiling and laughing, and it struck me that Tom and Ellen would make an ideal couple. They were both thorough, organized, and efficient. They took their duties seriously. Who was I kidding to think that a man like Tom Braddock would fall for someone like me? Ethan's rejection should have reminded me that no matter what I might look like on the outside, the woman on the inside wasn't desirable enough—or apparently wealthy enough—for the long term. How many times did I have to learn that lesson?

I looked down at my boots and kept my gaze focused on the trail for the rest of the hike.

❧❧❧❧❧

Ellen and Tom were still in the lead when we returned a little early to Selborne. Tom told us we had almost an hour to look around the village if we liked. There was a quaint post office that was more like the English-village version of a convenience store. There were also several small galleries and artist's cooperatives. I was all set to go shopping when Ellen pulled me over to the side.

"Let's offer to buy Mrs. Parrot a drink at the pub."

"Why?"

"Because I think she took the diary. And I'm going to get it back."

Before I could stop her, Ellen had sprung into action.

"Mrs. Parrot." Ellen stepped toward the older woman. "My sister and I were wondering if you might like to join us for something to drink in the pub garden."

The older woman's face lit up, as if she were truly happy to receive the invitation. "Yes, dear. That would be delightful."

She didn't look like someone who would sneak into Ellen's room intent on thievery, but then appearances could be deceiving, as I knew from personal experience. I didn't look like someone who had a brain in her head, but I wasn't the idiot most men took me to be. And I was holding out hope that Mrs. Parrot was the culprit, not Ethan. If Ellen thought she could get her to confess, then I was more than willing to help with the interrogation.

This pub, like the other ones we'd been to all week, boasted a low ceiling, heavy beams, and lots of charm.

"The garden's through there," Ellen said with a nod. "Why don't I get the drinks, and you two find us a table."

The rear of the pub boasted a cozy covered patio, but beyond that was a large garden with tables scattered under enormous trees. Several locals and their dogs had already settled in, but we found a table in the back corner in the shade.

"Have you been to Selborne often?" I asked Mrs. Parrot, more to fill the awkward silence than out of any real curiosity.

"On occasion. The garden at Gilbert White's house is very fine." We were scheduled to spend part of our afternoon there, a tour of the house followed by a walk up the famous zigzag path. Gilbert White and a friend had built it up the steep side of the hill, or hanger.

"Here we are." Ellen appeared balancing three large glasses. She set them on the table—diet sodas for us, and something that looked like cider for Mrs. Parrot.

I'd run out of small talk, so I let Ellen take the lead. She settled into her chair, took a sip of her soda, and then rested her clasped hands on the table.

"Mrs. Parrot, my sister and I have a dilemma, and we believe that you might be able to help us."

The older woman's face gave nothing away. "I should be delighted to help, if I can."

Ellen looked down at her hands and then back at Mrs. Parrot. "We've lost something. Something rather important."

"We can look through the van," Mrs. Parrot said, unruffled. "Perhaps underneath the seats . . ."

I couldn't take the dithering. "When my sister said 'lost,' she meant 'stolen.'"

"Mimi—"

I didn't have the patience to hint around. "Look, Mrs. P, here's the situation. When Ellen arrived at Oakley Hall, she was given a package with a very old book in it. A diary." I watched her intently for any sign of recognition or guilt.

"And it's gone missing?" Butter wouldn't have melted in her mouth, she was so cool.

"Actually, we think you stole it," I said.

"Mimi!" Ellen looked horrified.

"Well, it's true. Mrs. P here is the only one who could have cared about that diary." I turned to the older woman. "So we'd like it back, if you don't mind."

"I haven't got it."

My stomach dropped. She didn't say she didn't know what we were talking about, or that we were mistaken about the importance of the diary. She simply denied possessing it.

"Mimi, wait—"

I shushed Ellen and turned back to Mrs. Parrot. "You do know what we're talking about then?"

She paused for a moment and then nodded. "I do."

I shot Ellen a smug glance, and relief poured through me. The diary's disappearance wasn't my fault after all. "We don't want to have to involve the police," I said to the older woman.

"Of course you don't." Mrs. Parrot looked at Ellen, then back at me. "Not since that diary is stolen property to begin with."

"I didn't—" Ellen looked horrified.

"No, you didn't," Mrs. Parrot conceded. "But the person who gave it to you took what didn't belong to them."

I wasn't going to stand for that. "My mother would never—"

"Mimi!"

Mrs. Parrot smiled like the Cheshire Cat, fully satisfied with the mischief she'd wrought.

"Girls, I don't expect that you will believe me when I tell you I don't have the diary. I have no way to prove my innocence."

"My point exactly," I said under my breath, but they both heard me.

"As I said, I can't prove my innocence. But perhaps I can give you some reason to believe me when I tell you I don't have the diary in my possession."

"Why would we believe you?" I asked.

"Because if I had the diary, I would tell you straightaway."

"You're very confident," I said. "You really don't think we'd call the police if you confessed?"

"No, I don't. It would simply be my word against yours. And, my dears, you are the foreigners here." She smiled, but I didn't mistake the expression for humorous goodwill. No, it was definitely one hundred percent triumph.

"So who has it then, if you don't?" I asked.

My question did cause her serene expression to grow troubled. "Now that is a most vexing question. When was it taken?"

"Sometime yesterday while we were out," Ellen said. Her cheeks were flushed, but I didn't think it was from the heat. When we were kids, she used to turn red when she was hiding something.

"You would have been far better off to place it in the hotel safe." Mrs. Parrot turned the glass of cider in her hand. "I assume it was in your room?"

Ellen bristled. "I didn't want to alert anyone to its existence."

"But someone already knew."

Ellen sagged in her chair. "Honestly, I'm sick of the whole thing. All I wanted was to get this tour over with to meet the terms of Mom's will. I didn't ask for all this mystery and intrigue."

"So your mother did give you the diary?" Mrs. Parrot arched an eyebrow. "I suspected as much."

I looked at Mrs. Parrot, startled. "Why would you suspect it came from our mother?"

Mrs. Parrot paused for a long moment, as if she were gathering her thoughts and deciding which ones to make public. I had a feeling she did that a lot.

"I knew your mother when she lived in England."

A part of me wasn't surprised at that. After all, the Austen devotees were a close-knit circle.

"A lot of people knew my mother," Ellen said.

Mrs. Parrot wiped the moisture from the sides of her glass with her finger. "Your mother and I were both members of a certain . . . group."

"An Austen group?"

"A society, if you will. A rather secret one."

I rolled my eyes. "I think you're just making this up to cover up your theft."

She pursed her lips. "If I had the diary, I can assure you that I wouldn't still be here, with this tour. I would have made my excuses and returned to London."

A chill swept over me. Ethan had done just that. If Mrs. Parrot didn't have the diary, then . . .

"So why does it matter that you knew our mother? And that you both were in this secret society?" I said. I couldn't think about Ethan at that moment, or I would fall apart.

Mrs. Parrot gave us both a measuring look. "The group of which I'm speaking was called . . . is called, I should say, the Formidables."

"The Formidables?" It sounded like some pretentious group of rabid Austen fans.

Mrs. Parrot curled her hand around her glass. "It was the name Cassandra and Jane gave themselves. It was meant as a joke for their nieces and nephews. The formidable maiden aunts."

"It sounds bogus to me," I said.

"I can assure you that it isn't."

Ellen's jaw went tense. "Are you saying that our mother was one of these Formidables? Because I don't believe you. She would have told us. I mean, she couldn't keep quiet about anything having to do with Jane Austen, much less about a secret like that."

"I'm sure she didn't want the diary to be found," Mrs. Parrot said. "Something like that is very hard to keep a secret."

Ellen turned very pale.

"So what do you have, besides things like Cassandra's diary?" I asked Mrs. Parrot. "All the lost letters everyone's always nattering on about? The manuscripts of the novels? Secret portraits?"

"Yes," Mrs. Parrot said.

"Yes?" I looked at her skeptically. "You mean you have all that stuff?"

"Various members have the keeping of it, but if the whole collection were brought together, yes."

"And so now you want Cassandra's diary too."

"The Formidables have been looking for it for a number of years. It disappeared almost forty years ago." Mrs. Parrot's eyes grew cloudy with some strong emotion. "At the same time your mother left England."

"Maybe it belonged to her," I said. I wasn't about to let Mrs. Parrot cast aspersions on my mother's character.

"It did in a way. She was in charge of its keeping, but as to belonging... well, I would argue that it was the rightful property of the Formidables."

I rolled my eyes. "You make it sound so clandestine. I don't see what a bunch of Austen fans would have to hide."

"Don't you? After seeing the diary? Didn't you read it?"

"But shouldn't the world know about how Jane and Cassandra really interacted? What the sisters' relationship was really like?" I asked.

Mrs. Parrot shook her head. "Sometimes sisters do funny things for one another. Private things."

"So this diary, it's authentic?" Ellen asked. "It's really Cassandra Austen's diary?"

"It is."

My heart started to beat faster. "So you came on this tour on purpose?" I had to look at her with some newfound respect. "To get it back?" I had thought she was simply a dotty old academic.

"I hoped to convince you to return the diary to the Formidables."

"Well, we don't have it," Ellen said. "Not anymore."

"Plus, it's ours," I argued. "We have plans for it."

"Mimi—"

"We're going to sell it at auction."

"No, we're—"

Mrs. Parrot's expression grew severe. "You can't sell what you don't have, though, can you?"

"We'll find it." I was determined. A little thing like a missing diary was not going to stand between me and my boutique. "Why is it such a big deal to you guys, anyway?" I asked. "Who even cares about Cassandra's diary? It's not like it's Jane's."

"You don't know then, do you?" Mrs. Parrot dropped that mysterious hint and took a long drink of her cider.

"Know what?" I didn't trust her.

"That the diary is one of a pair."

"A pair." She had to be making this up.

"A matched set. Given to Cassandra and Jane Austen by their great-aunt, Leonora."

"So you simply want to bring the set back together?" Ellen asked. She looked far too trusting.

"No. It's not that simple."

"Are you telling me that somewhere out there, someone has Jane Austen's diary?" I wasn't an expert, but I knew enough to recognize the Holy Grail when someone described it to me.

"That would be . . . priceless." Ellen looked stunned. "It could provide so much information—"

"Which is precisely why we must find it and keep it safe," Mrs. Parrot said.

"Why do you keep it all secret?" I said. "Wouldn't it be better to give everyone access to it?"

Mrs. Parrot shook her head. "The Formidables were founded by Cassandra Austen for the very purpose of protecting Jane's privacy. Cassandra did this at her sister's request."

"But it doesn't make sense."

"It does, if one has a sister. Who better to understand the need to keep secrets?"

Ellen shot me a look, and I frowned. Mrs. Parrot did have a point.

"So you truly don't have Cassandra's diary?" I asked her. "Scout's honor?"

"I am not aware of what that sort of honor is, but if you're asking me to assure you of my truthfulness, then let me do so."

Ellen looked unconvinced. "What if we asked to meet some more of these . . . Formidables. Would you introduce us?"

"There's no reason to do so, not if you don't have the diary."

Touché. That round to Mrs. Parrot.

"Look," Ellen said, "we're both looking for the diary now. It makes more sense for us to pool our efforts."

I shot her a look, but she ignored me. It was one thing to confess to Ellen that I'd blabbed to Ethan. I didn't want to have to tell Mrs. Parrot as well.

"I would agree," Mrs. Parrot said, "except that if we should find the diary, we would have very different ends in mind for it." She looked at Ellen and then at me. "But perhaps we could come to an agreement."

"Good." Ellen looked at her watch. "It's time for lunch. Shall we join the others inside?"

We took our glasses with us, and I followed Ellen and Mrs. Parrot into the pub. My sister was up to something; I could tell. But I wasn't quite sure what it was.

CHAPTER
TWENTY-ONE

fter lunch, Ellen fell into step beside me as we walked from the pub down the lane to Gilbert White's house. Since the moment that Mrs. Parrot convinced me that she didn't have Cassandra's diary, I had known what I had to do. I had to tell Ellen the truth about spilling the beans to Ethan.

"She doesn't know about the riddles," Ellen said without preamble, before I could even begin to confess my misdeed.

"Oh." I hadn't thought of that. "But if we know more than she does, why did you offer—"

"Look, if she can help us find Cassandra's diary, we can get our hands on it long enough to double-check the riddles. Then she can have it."

"But we'll lose the diary."

"We'll lose *that* diary."

I was confused for a moment, and then comprehension dawned. "Because we know, now, what the clues lead to," I said. We shared a knowing smile.

"Jane's diary," Ellen said. "It has to be. Cassandra must have hidden it somewhere. Those riddles are the map to the treasure." She grinned at me. "We might lose the battle, but we'll win the war."

Jane Austen's diary. The bidding would be epic. "Are you really willing to try and sell it, if we find it?"

"I am now."

"What changed your mind?"

She hesitated. "I think Daniel has the diary."

"What?" But Ethan—

"Mom sent him on this tour to help us, but I think he decided to help himself to the diary instead. He's the only one who knew about it, other than Mrs. Parrot."

My heart sank. "Oh, Ell. You didn't tell me. I'm so sorry." Did that mean it hadn't been Ethan after all? At least my feelings for Ethan had met a quick demise, unlike Ellen's long-standing affection for Daniel. She walked beside me, her head held high, too high, and I could tell how much she was hurting.

"He never wanted me," she said. "I should have known that from the beginning."

I didn't know what to say, how to offer her any kind of comfort. I'd encouraged her to throw herself at him, and look how it had turned out.

Ellen stopped on the sidewalk and grabbed my arm. "I want you to have your dream, Meems. I do. I never meant to suggest otherwise. I just—"

"What?"

"I guess I was hoping you'd come back home to Dallas. That if you didn't have the money for the boutique, you'd have to."

"You wanted me to fail?"

"No." She shook her head. "I just wanted you to be my sister again."

"We don't have to sell it if we find it, you know," I said, but my words sounded pretty weak.

Ellen looped her arm through mine. "Actually, I think we do. Whatever we find, I think it should benefit both of us somehow."

"Only if you're sure." Because now that she was certain, I wasn't quite as much.

"I think the Austen sisters would understand," she replied, but I had my doubts. It sounded to me as if Cassandra and Jane Austen had gone to great lengths to protect each other, just as Ellen and I were beginning to do.

⚜⚜⚜⚜⚜

When we reached the Wakes, the home of Gilbert White, I lingered with the group while a docent gave a brief overview of the house and its famous occupant. I watched Mimi standing at the front of the group and felt a small stab of pride. She was holding her head up well in the wake of Ethan's defection. In the past, a romantic setback would have meant at least two days in bed with pints of Rocky Road and piles of Oreos.

The docent was still talking when I spied Daniel slipping out the side door into the garden. I followed him down the brick walk until we were far enough from the house not to be overheard.

"Daniel, wait. We need to talk." He wasn't going to get away that easily.

He turned to face me. "Ellen—"

"I want the truth, Daniel."

He shut his eyes for a moment, and when he opened them, I could see how troubled he was. "I should have told you the truth from the beginning."

"The truth?" This was it then. He had stolen the diary. I couldn't even look at him. I turned away and fought the desire to run into the garden just beyond where we stood.

"So what was the plan?" I said, biting off each word. I didn't need to hear his confession to know what he'd done. "Once you had me hooked, you'd convince me to turn it over to you?" I shook my head. "No, that couldn't have been it, because you got impatient and took it out of my room."

"What are you talking about?"

"The diary, of course. You took it, and now you're telling me you're sorry. Why?"

"Ellen, don't be ridiculous." His eyes narrowed. "I didn't take it. When did the diary go missing?"

"Like you don't know." Why was I even standing there?

"I didn't take it." Twin furrows etched his forehead, and he clenched his fist at his side. "I lied to you about something, yes, but I'm not a thief."

The first twinges of doubt squeezed my heart.

"You're the only one who knows about the diary besides me and Mimi." I decided not to mention Mrs. Parrot. "It had to be you."

His lips tightened into a thin line. "That's really what you think of me?"

And then understanding dawned. "It was you talking to Mrs. Parrot at the Vyne."

Slowly, with great reluctance, he nodded. "We thought you might have overheard us."

"You told her about it?"

"She already knew. Or guessed, anyway. I've run across Mrs. Parrot before in my business. My presence here made her suspicious that someone on the tour had something valuable."

"A Jane Austen kind of valuable."

"Yes."

Despite the hot breeze against my face, I shivered. "Why didn't you tell me?"

He took a step closer to me. "Because I was breaking a promise to you. But your mother hired me to help you. I wanted to pick Mrs. Parrot's brain, in a roundabout way."

"And did it work?"

He shrugged. "I didn't find out anything that I didn't already know."

Did he really expect me to believe him? "And what do you know? The diary's value on the open market?"

His shoulders stiffened. "I know that I care about you. I didn't just come here because your mother hired me. I came to see you, to find out if there was still that connection between us."

He paused, took a deep breath, and swallowed. "Look, Ell. I came here for you, not that stupid diary." He reached for my hands. "Nothing else. Just you."

I had waited so many years to hear those words, only now they didn't mean what they once would have.

"I don't believe you. I think you stole it."

His face turned white. "Are you seriously saying—"

"I haven't spent all these years nursing a broken heart just to throw it under your feet and watch you trample on it again."

"I never—"

"You did." I smiled ruefully through my tears. "You didn't mean to. But you did it all the same."

"Ellen—"

"I'm going to catch up with the group," I said and moved to step past him. He caught my arm.

"Don't throw this away, Ell."

I actually laughed. "The only thing I'm throwing away here, Daniel, is you."

I couldn't have hoped for a better exit line, so I took advantage of it. I shook off his hold and headed across the lawn, away from the house, thankful for the support of my hiking boots and the way they made me feel as if I mastered the ground with each step. I needed something to make me feel that way.

"Ellen . . . "

The wind carried Daniel's voice behind me. I hoped he wouldn't follow me, because already my cheeks were awash with tears, and my nose was starting to run.

I reached the back of the lawn and darted up a path into the woods. Then I stopped and dug a bandanna out of my pack. It was stiff with perspiration, but I still managed to wipe my eyes and blow my nose. The heat would account for my flushed and disheveled state. I was not about to give anyone any reason to suspect that I was upset.

My face restored, I slung my pack over my shoulder and went to find the group.

CHAPTER
TWENTY-TWO

he sisterly camaraderie that Mimi and I had established lasted through the remainder of the afternoon. Later, the van and the taxi ferried us from Selborne into Winchester and deposited us at our final destination, the Hotel du Vin.

I couldn't believe that the tour was almost over. We had the farewell dinner that evening, a tour of Winchester in the morning, and then Tom would drop us off at the train station.

Mimi and I agreed to settle in and then meet in the hotel's garden before we dressed for dinner. She hadn't pressed me to tell her about what had happened with Daniel, but as we sat at a table beneath a large umbrella, the musical sound of flowing water soothing us, I spilled the events of the afternoon.

Mimi's eyes widened. "Here you have the man you've always loved, traveling across an ocean to win you, and all you can think is that he's after the diary?"

"What else am I supposed to think?" He hadn't exactly been truthful.

Mimi gave me a stern look. "Tell me what he said. Exactly."

"He said that Mom contacted him and asked him to come on the tour so that he could help us with returning the diary."

"And?"

"He said that he agreed, but just as an excuse to see me again."

"That's bad because why?"

I sighed. "What if he's the one who stole the diary?"

Mimi leaned forward. "What if he's not?" She stopped and bit her lip. "You can't afford to be wrong about this. Because if Daniel didn't take the diary, then you're throwing away happiness with both hands."

That kept me quiet for a long moment.

"Look, Ellen," Mimi said, "heaven knows that I'm no expert at romance. I mean, my week hasn't exactly been a relationship success. But don't send Daniel packing because he made a mistake by tipping off Mrs. Parrot." She paused. "Or are you still holding Melissa against him?"

"I admit it. I want to be the only woman he's ever loved."

"So your feelings aren't exactly unconditional. Is your pride really worth giving up love?"

"You think I'm crazy to tell Daniel to leave me alone."

"Crazy? That's debatable." She smiled, and I felt a faint echo of a smile on my own lips. "But foolish? Yes." She paused. "For so long, I've thought we were complete opposites, but we're not. We both fell into the same trap—trying to find a love that's perfect. There's no such thing."

I wasn't used to Mimi being the font of wisdom in our relationship. "Of course there's no such thing."

"We know that intellectually. But Mom infected us with her Jane Austen adoration."

I looked around at the beautiful garden. "So where does that leave us?" I asked.

"I think it leaves us right where we started."

"On Sunday, you mean, when we arrived at Oakley Hall?"

Mimi shook her head. "No. I mean it leaves us right back at that little house in Dallas with Mom. Wondering if we'll ever find Mr. Right."

"No way," I said. "No more Mr. Right talk, ever."

"What about Mr. Maybe?"

"Not even that. If nothing else, I've realized that romance and I don't mix."

"I don't think Daniel would agree."

"I thought you said we were starting over." Mimi could worry a subject like a dog could a bone when she put her mind to it. "Daniel is in the past."

"I didn't say we were starting over. I said we were right back where we started. There's a big difference."

"I don't understand."

Mimi looked at me. Really looked at me. "We have a chance to do it right this time, Ellen. The blinders have come off. We might have worn different styles, but we both had them on. Now, I think, we can see our lives differently."

To be honest, I wasn't sure I wanted to see my life any way but as the same comfortable old rut I'd left when I came to England.

"What if it's too late?" I said, trying not to let the panic I felt seep into my voice. "Maybe we've missed our chance."

Mimi frowned. "That's the point, Ell. Maybe we get more than one chance."

I could tell she was thinking of Tom. "And it's different for you this time?" I couldn't help the note of disbelief in my voice.

Mimi actually blushed. "Yes," she said in a strong, clear voice. "I think it is."

Tom Braddock was hardly the knight in shining armor that Mimi had always talked about, but he was a good man. A strong man. A man who adored my sister.

A sudden burst of loneliness washed over me.

"Give Daniel another chance," Mimi said. "If we find out he took the diary, all bets are off. But I don't think he did."

"You sound so sure."

She shook her head. "I'm not sure of anything. Not anymore. But . . . " She grimaced. "Look, sis, I'd bet my last dollar that Daniel's not our culprit."

"Then who is?"

"I don't know. But if I were you, I'd trust Daniel. Don't let your jealousy over Melissa ruin things between you two."

"I'll think about it." An easy enough promise to keep. I'd done little but think about Daniel for the past five days. "It would just be a lot easier if I knew where that diary was."

Mimi stood up. "Come on. We need to get ready for the farewell dinner." She took off across the garden, almost as if she were running from something. I glanced around, thinking that I might see Ethan lurking somewhere, but there was no sign of him.

No doubt it was simply her frustration with me. I'd watched her throw away a good thing often enough to know how difficult a spectator sport that could be.

❦❦❦❦❦

Mimi loaned me a dress for the farewell dinner. The Mediterranean-blue chiffon had a deep V-neck, left my shoulders bare, and fell to the floor in soft pleats. I hoped it wasn't too dressy, but Mimi convinced me to go for it.

Mimi's advice to me in the garden was having an effect. She was right, of course. No matter how much I'd tried not to be contaminated by my mother's Austen obsession, I hadn't avoided absorbing the idea of the perfect man being out there somewhere, if I could just find him. Or manage not to lose him. Daniel had shown himself to be imperfect, and that had scared me far more than the idea that he might have taken the diary.

Was I willing to take a chance on an imperfect man? Or would I rather revel in my righteous indignation over his failure to live up to my inflated expectations?

We returned to Chawton Great House for the final dinner. Tom had said it would be the perfect venue for our last meal together, and he was right. The dark-paneled dining room was virtually unchanged from Austen's day. The long table and chairs had actually belonged to Jane's brother Edward. Now it was fully set with beautiful china, sparkling crystal, shining silver, and centerpieces of enormous roses from the garden.

"Jane herself would have eaten off this table," Tom said with a grin, and all of us made appreciative noises. We all laughed, too, when several of the ladies took turns sitting in various chairs to see if they could "sense" her presence.

The staff offered us small glasses of sherry before dinner, and I felt both glamorous and apprehensive. Daniel had been eyeing me since the ride over from Winchester, but he hadn't approached me yet. Tom and Mimi seemed as standoffish with each other as Daniel and I did, but I was determined not to interfere. There was no sign of Ethan, and I felt relieved on Mimi's behalf.

I moved to a window that overlooked the front drive. The village church sat just at the gate to the house, its spire peeping out above the trees.

Daniel came up to stand beside me. "Are there any views in England that you couldn't put on a postcard?" he said with a nod toward the church.

"I think it's a legal requirement," I said with a smile. I didn't really think he had stolen the diary. I didn't think it was

Mrs. Parrot now, either. Which left me with no idea whatsoever as to whom the culprit might be.

"Ellen, I wanted to apologize again for violating your trust."

"I should apologize too." I couldn't quite look him in the eye. "I was . . . hurt."

"I should have told you I wanted to talk to Mrs. Parrot."

I held up a hand. "You don't have to explain. I think I understand. Or at least I'm beginning to."

"I'd always wondered, if I saw you again—"

"Don't."

He grimaced. "Don't apologize? Don't talk to you? Which is it?"

"The first. As to the second, I think we actually have quite a lot of talking to do."

"We do?" He breathed a literal sigh of relief. "I'm glad to hear it."

I glanced around the room. "Not here though. Let's sneak out for a few minutes."

He glanced at his watch. "Dinner won't be for a little while yet. Come on."

I saw Tom notice our departure, but he didn't stop us. We slipped out of the house and headed around the side toward the rose garden we'd seen two days before. Neither of us said anything until we came to a stop on the terrace just outside the garden.

Daniel took my hand in his, and my pulse raced. "I have a confession to make," he said.

"Another one?" His words did nothing to slow my heart rate.

"Back in college, I knew that you were in love with me."

I started to pull away, but he kept a gentle grip on my hand. "Daniel—"

"I think that I was in love with you too. But I was just a kid. I didn't know how to handle it."

"You don't have to—"

"Shh." He leaned toward me, and his lips brushed mine. "We'll figure all that out later. Right now, let's just concentrate on this."

I should have argued, but I didn't. We still had the diary's mysterious disappearance to solve, but for the moment, this was enough. Daniel's lips on mine and the scent of roses and hope heavy in the evening air.

⚜⚜⚜⚜⚜

I had hoped that Ethan would turn up for the farewell dinner, but Tom said he was still in London, as far as anyone knew. I'd known as Ellen and I sat in the hotel garden that afternoon that I had to figure out a way to get the diary back. Because of my misplaced trust in Ethan—not to mention my romantic desperation—I had made a major error in judgment. Now it was up to me to rectify it.

After we returned to the hotel from the farewell dinner, Ellen said that she was ready for bed and headed upstairs to her room. But from the starry look in her eyes, I expected she would spend more time mooning over Daniel than actually sleeping.

I returned to my room, slipping out of my evening gown and taking off my makeup, but when I lay down on the bed, I was still wide awake. I couldn't blame my sleeplessness on the heat. My room was lovely and cool with the night breeze stealing through the open window, but it didn't make me any less restless. I tried a long, bubbly soak in the enormous bathtub, but my mind wouldn't disengage. That wasn't a problem I normally had, to be honest. I had always been driven more by emotion than intellect. The events of the week, though, had me wound up tight.

I pulled on jeans and a T-shirt and made my way quietly out of my room, down the stairs, and into the bar. I didn't see anyone from our tour among the locals scattered at various tables. I ordered an Orangina and slipped out into the side garden. Perhaps a little night air would do the trick.

The outdoor tables were deserted, but I could smell cigar smoke coming from the bothy, a small shelter in the side garden where the gentlemen could indulge. It was difficult to see inside, since the low-hanging roof built to contain the smoke blocked anyone sitting there from view. I could see, though, a pair of expensive Italian leather loafers polished to a high sheen. My heart raced. If Ethan had returned, it was time to confront him.

I ducked through the opening and then stopped. Low-slung leather armchairs circled the small space. Candles flickered on the occasional tables tucked between the chairs. The lone occupant wasn't Ethan after all. It was Tom.

"Mimi? Are you okay?"

"Um, yeah. I'm fine. I just—"

"I find it difficult to unwind at the end of a tour," he said with gentle understanding. He nodded toward the chair next to him. "If you're not offended by cigar smoke, you're welcome to join me."

I decided that the company would be worth putting up with the smell. "Okay."

"Are you a big cigar smoker?" I asked when I settled into the chair next to him.

He made a face. "Only occasionally. When I'm restless." He shrugged. "I gave up cigarettes years ago, but every once in a while, I still indulge."

"To unwind."

"Among other things."

I decided not to ask what those other things were. He seemed like a man with a lot on his mind.

"Thank you for a wonderful week," I said. I set my Orangina on the table next to his cigar. "Obviously I'm not the usual walking-tour type, but I've really enjoyed it."

"Blisters and all?"

"Especially the 'and all.'" Which encompassed a lot. Sisterly strife. Disappointed romantic hopes and semipublic humiliation. Secrecy, theft, duplicity . . .

"So you're not sorry you came?" He was looking at me with that intent gaze, and I could tell that our conversation that morning in the lythe hadn't been any easier on him than it had been on me.

"No. I guess I owe my mother a 'thank you.'" Which Ellen and I would show her when we decided the next day where to scatter her ashes. We still hadn't picked a spot.

Tom rested his hands on his knees in a military-looking posture. "I owe her one too."

I looked up at him, and I found myself at a complete loss for words. He was so different from Ethan. Not the romantic ideal I'd spent so many years pursuing, but something far more . . . real.

"She's the one who designed the tour, you know." Tom placed his elbows on the arms of the chair and loosely clasped his fingers in front of him.

"My mother?"

"It was meant to be a surprise."

I paused. "I didn't know." I didn't want to cry—not in front of Tom. I forced myself to smile, but the tears still sprang to my eyes. "You said it was someone who'd been at school with the owner of the company. It must have been an old friend of hers in England."

"I only had contact with her by e-mail," Tom said, "but she seemed like a fine woman."

I sniffed back tears, but then I smiled. "She was."

"Mimi—"

"I was hoping for a grand romance when I came on this tour." I stopped, unsure whether I had the courage to continue.

"Did you find one?" He didn't look disturbed by my abrupt change of subject.

I should have minded the smell of his cigar, but with both of us nestled in the bothy, the pungent smoke perfumed the air in a very masculine way.

"I think so. I hope so." Why did his question make my pulse pick up speed?

"So what will you do now?"

"I don't know." The only thing I did know was that I wasn't ready to go home.

He paused, but he didn't reach for the cigar. "Would you consider staying here to sort out your future?"

Now I knew why my heart was racing. "Stay here in England? Just like that?"

"Well, there might be one or two complications to deal with."

"Like the fact that I'd have no job and no place to live," I said ruefully.

He leaned forward, reached for my hand, and twined my fingers with his. "Not exactly."

"What do you mean 'not exactly'?"

He was breathtakingly handsome. His strong jaw, stormy silver-blue eyes, and silvered hair were all straight out of a BBC Jane Austen adaptation. Give him riding breeches and a cravat, and women would swoon. I would swoon. As a matter of fact, I was in the act of swooning. My knees went distinctly weak.

"The main problem I see," Tom said as he lifted the other hand to cup my cheek, "is how we're going to break it to Ellen that you're not going home with her."

He leaned forward and brushed his lips against mine. You could hardly even have called it a kiss, but it drew me to the edge of my chair, seeking closer contact with him.

I launched myself into his arms. He caught me and pulled me into his lap. Then he kissed me properly. Thoroughly. Like an Austen hero kisses his lady, with passion but also a hint of restraint. I was pretty sure the bothy hadn't been intended for this purpose, but in a pinch . . .

"I think that I love you," I breathed into his ear when we came up for air. The words startled me. I hadn't known they were true until the moment I said them.

"It took you long enough." Tom smiled down at me with a kind of fierce, masculine happiness. Not exuberant, but deep-seated and purposeful.

"It hasn't even been a week," I said, laughing. "Give a girl a chance."

"It only took me the first five minutes," he said smugly.

"Military efficiency, huh?" I pressed a kiss against his neck.

"No." I leaned back to see that his smile had faded. The intensity in his gaze turned my insides to mush. "More like the answer to a prayer."

How could I not be humbled by that? "I don't deserve you." I wasn't fishing for compliments or reassurance. I knew at that moment, deep in my bones, the truth of that statement.

"I waited for you for so many years," I said. I wrapped a hand around his neck and pulled him forward so I could kiss him again. "What took you so long?"

His arms came around me, strength and experience and wisdom enveloping me.

"I got here as soon as I could," he whispered before, once again, we put the privacy in the bothy to good use.

CHAPTER

TWENTY-THREE

 couldn't believe it was the last day of
the tour. The week had gone by so
quickly, and yet it seemed ages since
Ellen and I had turned up at Oakley
Hall on Sunday evening. I had run out of time to figure out how
to get the diary back from Ethan. I couldn't avoid telling Ellen
the truth any longer. Before we left Winchester, I had to come
clean with her and ask for her help in fixing my mistake.

Tom rounded us up on the hotel steps that morning. "We'll
see the house on College Street where Jane Austen was living
when she died, and then walk over to the cathedral to visit her
grave and the exhibit about her life."

"Will we get to go inside the house?" someone asked, but
Tom shook his head.

"It's a private residence now. The owner understandably
gets a bit irritated at people knocking on his front door, asking
for a tour."

That drew smiles and a few laughs from the group.

"After we finish at the cathedral, we'll return here for our luggage and head for the train station."

With that, Tom took off down the street, and we obediently followed as we'd been doing all week. We made our way through a few narrow twists and turns, following Tom's instructions to watch for cars jumping out from behind the sharp corners. Finally we crossed one last street, and suddenly, through the trees, the cathedral loomed in front of us.

The enormous stone structure somehow managed to look delicate as well as majestic. Tom paused on the square outside so we could take photographs, but then he led us around the side of the building, past a small lawn where workers were assembling large stage lights.

"What's happening here?" Tom asked a woman who was passing by. She had the scarlet academic gown of a teacher from Winchester College thrown over one arm.

"They're presenting *Romeo and Juliet*," she said with a smile.

I looked up at the massive side of the cathedral, with its magnificent buttresses and intricate stonework. "It's the perfect backdrop." There was even a small parapet in the corner that would serve quite nicely as Juliet's balcony.

Farther on, we came to a collection of Tudor buildings hunched over the street. A group of schoolboys in white choir robes passed by, and Tom explained that it was most likely the end of the term for nearby Winchester College, the boys' boarding school, and they were headed to the cathedral for a closing service. It all seemed quite magical.

We stuck to the pavement rather than the cobblestoned street and a few turns later found ourselves in front of a brick townhouse painted a vibrant yellow. Tom gathered us on the pavement opposite where a small bit of lawn was buffered by a high wall. I suspected it was either part of the cathedral grounds or part of the college.

Ellen, Daniel, and I were standing to the back of the group as Tom relayed the details about the last months of Jane Austen's life, her wasting illness, and how Cassandra cared for her. They had traveled to Winchester so that the ailing Jane could be near her doctor. Ellen and I had heard most of the story from our mother, and so we spoke in whispers as we gazed at the house.

"It seems sad, doesn't it?" Ellen asked me. "For her not to be at home when she died."

"It does." I drew a deep breath. I had to bite the bullet and tell my sister the truth about how I'd betrayed her trust. "Ellen, there's something I need to tell—"

But Ellen was already saying something. "Look at the Dutch tourists." She pointed at a group moving toward us, no doubt eager to take our places on the small lawn so that they, too, could pay homage.

My courage failed me. "Very blond, aren't they?"

She nudged me. "You'd fit right in." It was the kind of lighthearted moment that had been missing in our relationship. I couldn't bring myself to spoil it.

We returned to the cathedral, and Tom led us through the entrance. The interior was practically empty of people, which was, as far as I was concerned, the best way to see such a magnificent building. Tom led us into the nave and gave us a brief history of the place before turning us loose to explore on our own.

"Let's go find her grave," Ellen whispered, tugging on my arm.

As it turned out, we had to make our way around the outer aisles of the cathedral in a large loop and were almost back to where we'd started before we found what we'd come to see.

The whole place was filled with memorials, of course, everything from very plain marble plaques inscribed with the details of the person's life and death to elaborate statues of royal and nearly royal personages. None of those memorials, though, prepared me for the large black slab that I now found at my feet, or the inscription on it.

In Memory of JANE AUSTEN, youngest daughter of the late Revd GEORGE AUSTEN, formerly Rector of Steventon in this County. She departed this Life on the 18th of July 1817, aged 41, after a long illness supported with the patience and the hopes of a Christian. The benevolence of her heart, the sweetness of her temper, and the extraordinary endowments of her mind obtained the regard of all who knew her and the warmest love of her intimate connections. Their grief is in proportion to their affection, they know their loss to be irreparable, but in their deepest affliction they are consoled by a firm though humble hope that her charity, devotion, faith and purity have rendered her soul acceptable in the sight of her REDEEMER.

❦❦❦❦❦

I hadn't thought I would cry, but my throat closed up, and I wanted to weep. For the first time on the trip, I felt my mother's presence, almost as if she were standing next to me. But no, that was Mimi, who looked as emotional as I felt.

"It doesn't even say anything about her writing," she protested. "Why wouldn't they mention that?"

I knew the answer from one of my mother's long-ago lectures on the subject. "Her novels were published anonymously in her lifetime. The only reason she got buried here was because of her father and all the clergymen in their family."

"It figures," Mimi said. "Write six of the greatest novels in the English language, but in the end, they only care who your male relatives were."

"Since when did you think that she wrote six of the greatest novels in the English language?" I asked, half laughing and half serious. Mom had spent years trying to get both of us to make our way through Jane Austen's entire oeuvre. She'd eventually succeeded with me, but I didn't know that Mimi had ever succumbed.

"I just finished *Sense and Sensibility*."

"When?"

And now she began to cry in earnest. "I started when Mom got sick."

"Mimi, what's wrong?" We'd been through all of this, and I thought we'd resolved it. "I don't blame you anymore. I understand why you couldn't come to Dallas."

"It's not that." She wiped at her eyes with the back of her hand. "It's the diary."

"The diary?"

"It's my fault that it's missing."

"What do you mean?"

"I might have mentioned it to Ethan."

My stomach dropped to the memorial beneath my feet. "Meems, you didn't."

"I thought that maybe he could help. He's related to the Austens, and he had a whole room full of that kind of thing. I wouldn't let him see it, though, until I'd told you and"— she choked back a sob—"that's why he dumped me. Because I wouldn't prove that I had the diary. But it didn't matter, because now he's taken it . . . "

I leaned forward and pulled her into my arms. "Shh, Mimi. It's okay."

She was crying so hard now that she shook. "We can't get it back now though. He'll never admit that he has it, and we don't have any proof."

I wanted to be mad at her, but she was trembling like a leaf, and suddenly that diary seemed like the least important thing in the world.

"Ellen, you have to forgive me." She pulled out of my arms. "I know it's practically a full-time job with me, but I really need for you to do that."

I looked at Mimi, the only family I had left in the world, and I knew that it was time to let go of the past. All of it. I wasn't going to get the magically perfect sister. Ever. But I wasn't going to be the perfect sister, either. Cassandra and Jane hadn't seen each other that way, and yet they'd been so devoted to one another. Mimi said I had to forgive her, and she was right. I could only hope that she could forgive me as well, for all the times I had let her down.

On impulse, I put my arm around my sister, and we stared down at the inscription. "Meems," I said, "do you think we could agree to make a new start? Right here, right now?"

She was quiet for a moment, and my chest tightened. Maybe it was too late. I'd held her at arm's length for so long. I'd judged her and fussed at her and generally made my contempt for her clear. I'd always thought the problem was that Mimi needed to make amends to me, but now I saw the situation in a different light.

"I am sorry, sis," I said and squeezed her shoulders. "We should have been able to talk about everything that happened with Mom."

"And I'm sorry that I wasn't there. I'm sorry I wasn't stronger."

"We still have to decide what to do with her ashes," I said. "We've gotten so caught up in all this diary stuff that I think we may have forgotten the most important reason that we're here."

"To say good-bye to Mom."

"And to pick her final resting place." I looked down at the memorial. "It's too bad we can't leave her here. That would probably have been her first choice."

The corners of Mimi's mouth turned up, just a little bit. "Well, if we can't leave her with Jane, maybe we could do the next best thing."

"Which would be?"

"To leave her with Cassandra."

I nodded. "In the churchyard at Chawton."

"Tom would probably drive us over there."

She turned toward me then, and we held on to each other while we both cried. Other tourists passing by probably took us for Jane Austen aficionados who were just a little too enmeshed in idol worship. Only Mimi and I knew what it had taken to bring us to this moment. Being named after the Dashwood sisters. A lifetime of misunderstandings. Our mother's manipulation from beyond the grave. And two real-life sisters who, two hundred years ago, had been far wiser about resolving their differences than we had been.

Mimi pulled back and laughed through her tears. "We look like fangirls, don't we, weeping at Jane Austen's grave."

I laughed through my tears. "Mom would be so proud." And that was the truth.

❧❧❧❧❧

Ellen still had her arm around me as we made our way out of the cathedral and met the others in front of the building.

"Ell, we've got to find Jane's diary," I said as we walked toward a low stone wall along the walkway to the gift shop. The sky was a somber gray. Fitting, given everything that had happened.

"We'll find it," Ellen said.

"Not for the money. I don't mean that."

"I know you don't."

"For mom."

Ellen nodded. "Do you think she knew about Jane's diary?"

I sighed. "I don't know. If we could just figure out the clues . . . " I let my words trail off, because Mrs. Parrot stepped up next to us.

"Girls, if I could have a moment."

"Ell, I think it's time to tell her," I said. "Daniel should be part of this too."

Mrs. Parrot's eyebrows arched. "Tell me what?"

"Just a moment," Ellen said. She stepped away toward the group and then returned with Daniel in tow.

"When we told you about the diary," I said to Mrs. Parrot, "we left a little bit out."

"How little was this bit?" She pursed her lips.

"We figured out that there were clues in Cassandra's diary," I said. "Riddles, of sorts, that may lead us to Jane's diary."

"And?"

"All we got were these random words. We're not even sure we have the right words."

"And they were?" Mrs. Parrot leaned forward.

"*Clothes* or *clothing*," I said. "Either *squeeze* or maybe *press*. And *school*. Oh, and also *road*. Or at least we think it's *road*. It might be *street*." It didn't sound like very impressive sleuthing when I said it out loud like that.

Mrs. Parrot frowned. "Are you certain?"

"No," Ellen snapped. "That's the problem, isn't it?" I knew she was frustrated.

"I have the riddles here somewhere." I slipped off my pack and dug through it until I found the now well-worn piece of hotel stationery. I handed it to Mrs. Parrot, who donned her thick glasses to study it. Daniel peered at it over her shoulder.

"I see." She looked up at us. "Why didn't you tell me this before?"

Ellen didn't even flinch. "Because we didn't trust you." She glanced at Daniel. "Either of you."

"And now you do?" Mrs. Parrot looked more intrigued than offended.

"Now we don't have any choice. Not if we're going to figure out what these clues mean."

Mrs. Parrot handed the paper back to me and then put her hand to her chin in the time-honored "thinking" pose. "*Clothes. Road. School. Press.*"

"It doesn't make any sense," I said. "Have you ever heard of a clothes road? Maybe it means some kind of printer's press."

And then Mrs. Parrot looked up at us.

"College Street," she said.

Goose bumps broke out up and down my arms. "The house where she was staying before she died."

"What about the other clues?" Ellen's voice was tight with emotion. "*Clothes* and *press*."

Mrs. Parrot looked at Ellen and Daniel, then at me. "That's quite straightforward, my dears. A clothespress is another name for a wardrobe."

"Are you saying it's in that house?" Daniel looked at Mrs. Parrot with interest. "We'll never get inside. Tom told us how much the owner hates being disturbed by the hordes of Austen followers."

Mrs. Parrot slipped her glasses from her face and wiped the lenses on the scarf draped over her substantial bosom. "I doubt that a two-hundred-year-old piece of furniture would still be in the same place," she said. "It was most certainly sold or given away long ago. These were only rented lodgings, you know, when Jane and Cassandra were here."

Ellen's shoulders slumped. "Then we'll never find it. It could be anywhere."

"What does it matter? We don't even know who the house belonged to back then." I couldn't believe we'd hit such a dead end.

"That we can find out easily enough," Mrs. Parrot said. "If the clothespress was part of a larger estate sale, like the one at Steventon when Mr. Austen retired, there might be a notice in the local paper listing the items." She looked at Daniel. "I believe you might be of some help with that, young man."

"I believe I might." He grinned.

It was a faint hope, but at this point, I would take any sliver of a possibility, no matter how small.

Ellen wasn't as quick to latch on to that faint hope though. "It's like looking for a needle in a haystack. Impossible."

"The Formidables have a tremendous network of resources, my dear." Mrs. Parrot looked quite determined. "We still stand a chance. No doubt it will take time, but—"

"If that clothespress still exists, it's either a family heirloom or an antique in someone's collection, right?" A faint memory glimmered at the back of my mind. It flickered, and I tried not to grab hold of it too strongly so that I wouldn't snuff it out. "You said it's like a wardrobe, right?"

"Yes, only smaller, most likely," Daniel said. "Not one of those monstrosities like in those Narnia tales."

"Would it be plain, or would it have some sort of design on it?" My heart started beating faster.

"It might be decorated," Daniel said. "With an Asian design. Chinese or Japanese. Japanned cabinets were very popular."

"I've seen one." The words just slipped out. "I think I know where Jane's diary is."

Ellen looked as though she couldn't decide whether to believe me or shoot me. "How could you possibly know where that particular clothespress is? It could be anywhere."

"Because I've seen it."

"At Chawton? In the cottage or the library?"

"No, it's at Deane."

"At Deane?" Daniel looked skeptical. "In the pub?"

I smiled then. Because at least my humiliation at the hands of Ethan would have some benefit. "No. It's at Ethan's house."

"Ethan's house?" Ellen's jaw dropped.

I nodded. "In one of the guest rooms. With all the other Austen artifacts."

"But how do you know it's the right one?" Ellen frowned, and I knew she was afraid to get her hopes up.

"He said his mother inherited the house after she married into the Austen family. All of the furnishings came with it."

"Just because it was in the family doesn't mean it's the one with the diary," Daniel warned.

"No. But something Ethan said at the time made me curious."

"Yes?" Mrs. Parrot was on high alert.

"He said it was owned by Jane Austen's niece, Fanny Knight."

"The one whose father owned Chawton Great House?" Ellen asked.

"Of course." Mrs. Parrot nodded with satisfaction. "Cassandra might have hidden the diary there, after Jane's death. For some reason she left it behind or couldn't retrieve it."

"So she could have had her brother track down the wardrobe and buy it," Daniel said.

"Did her brother or Fanny even know what was hidden in it?" Ellen asked.

Mrs. Parrot shook her head. "One can never account, of course, for the carelessness in large families. Somehow the secret was lost. Perhaps Fanny was afraid to entrust anyone with the knowledge. Or perhaps she never realized the clues were in Cassandra's diary. If she even had it."

"Look," I said, "Ethan's clothespress is the best lead we've got. I say we go over there and check it out."

"How are we going to do that?" Ellen asked.

Daniel smiled. "I have an idea."

e'll show up unan-
nounced," Daniel said
as we piled into the van.
He had wanted to take
off for Ethan's immediately, but Mrs. Parrot pointed out that we
needed Tom and the van. We couldn't have either until the tour
concluded and Tom dropped everyone else at the train station.

So Ellen, Mrs. Parrot, Daniel, and I were left to twiddle
our thumbs at the hotel for what seemed like an eternity but
was really less than an hour. At long last, Tom returned, and
we climbed into the van. I filled him in on everything that had
happened as we drove back to Deane, and then we hatched our
plan.

Tom and Mrs. Parrot would wait for us at the pub down the
road from Ethan's house, while Daniel, Ellen, and I tried to get
inside the house on the pretext of Daniel's professional interest

in some of the antiques that I'd mentioned seeing. I dreaded seeing Ethan again, and I didn't know whether such a crazy plan would work, but we had to try.

"If he doesn't want to show us the Austen stuff, you and I will distract him," Daniel said to me as Tom pulled the van to a stop in front of the pub. "Your sister can slip away to search for that clothespress."

I quickly gave Ellen directions to the guest room where I remembered seeing the clothespress. It had been late and dark, and I had been exhausted, so I wasn't sure how accurate my description was. Ellen assured me she would find the diary, no matter what.

Something was bothering me, though, in addition to feeling creepy about returning to Ethan's. Yes, I did feel a little bit like a woman scorned, but I was also uncomfortable with the idea of simply taking the diary out from under his nose. I was pretty sure my mother wouldn't have approved, but Mrs. Parrot knew more about the provenance of the diary than I did. I trusted her to know what was right.

We walked up the lane, since we didn't want Ethan to see the touring-company van. I led Daniel and Ellen around the side of the house to the parking area and then through the gate into the garden.

"Hello?" I called. There was no sign of the workmen Ethan had mentioned. "Is anyone home?"

The kitchen door opened, and Ethan stepped out. He ran a hand through his hair. "Um, hello. This is a surprise."

Daniel stepped forward. "We missed you on the tour. Tom said that business called you back to London. We took a chance that you might be here."

Ethan looked confused. "Kind of you to come to say good-bye, but really not necessary."

I stepped forward, my cheeks hot as fire. "Actually, I was telling Daniel about some of your antiques. He's a dealer, you know, and he thought he might be interested in looking to buy, if you were thinking of selling anything."

"Well, I hadn't really planned to—"

"Could he at least look? Then if you decide later that you do want to sell, he'll know what he was interested in buying."

As we'd hoped, Ethan's greed got the better of him. "Of course. I'd be delighted to give you the tour." He didn't look as if he trusted us, but he was too greedy to take a chance that Daniel wasn't really looking to buy.

Ethan motioned for us to follow him through the kitchen doorway. I hung back and let the others go first. After all, I had already seen the glories of Ethan's fabulous house.

Ethan led Daniel through the various rooms, and Ellen and I followed. Ethan paused to point out the paintings and furniture that might be of interest to Daniel, who made appreciative comments. Daniel's approval fed Ethan's ego. I could almost see his chest swelling. But there was no mention of the Austen room or the family heirlooms, and Daniel and I exchanged a frustrated glance. By the time we arrived on the terrace in the rear of the house, Ethan and Daniel were acting like the best of friends, but I began to fear that this plan wasn't going to work. Ethan hadn't led us anywhere near the guest room or the clothespress. Not even so much as an Austen-related pen nib.

In the corner of the terrace, a table stood beneath the shelter of a mammoth hanging wisteria. "Please stay for a cup of tea," Ethan said. He pulled out a chair for me, and Daniel did the same for Ellen. "If it won't bore you ladies too much, Daniel and I can discuss business."

Ethan disappeared into the kitchen and returned a few minutes later with a tea tray. Now if we could just create some sort of distraction to get Ellen back in the house while Daniel and I kept Ethan occupied.

❧❧❧❧❧

Mimi was about as subtle as a sledgehammer, the way her eyes kept shooting daggers at me. What she couldn't see, seated so close to Ethan, was that he was watching the rest of us like a hawk. I had the strangest feeling that he knew exactly why we were there.

My chance finally came when Ethan served the tea. I knew what I had to do, but it was going to be excruciating. I held the cup close to my lips, listened to the drone of conversation to make sure I'd picked the right moment, and with one quick flick of my wrist, dumped most of the contents of my cup into my lap.

"*Owww!*" I leaped to my feet. I wasn't a complete idiot. I'd made sure my napkin was positioned to soak up as much of the spill as I could. I snatched the napkin away, flung it beneath the table, and turned my back to its occupants.

"Ellen! Are you okay?" Mimi must have leaped to her feet in one flying movement, because she was instantly beside me. Tears burned my eyes. I hadn't meant to stage quite so authentic a catastrophe. But it would be worth it if I could locate that diary.

"I'm fine. I just need to find a bathroom . . . " I let my voice trail off on a teary note, which was entirely real.

"Ethan?" Mimi looked over her shoulder at him. "I can show her where it is, if you don't mind."

He was on his feet too. "Of course. Do you remember the way?"

"I can manage." Mimi took my hand and led me through the terrace doors and into the house before Ethan could offer to guide us. She stopped me a few feet inside. "You're a braver woman than I am. You didn't have to be quite so . . . dedicated to the cause."

"Can we just find the bathroom?" I said. "This really does burn."

Mimi might not have had a memory for birthdays or when it was her turn to do the dishes, but she made her way to the guest bathroom without a single wrong turn. She ushered me inside and closed the door.

"The room with the clothespress is right next door. I'll keep Ethan occupied as long as I can." She reached up on a shelf above the sink and handed me a small towel. Then she frowned. "Where will you hide it if you find it?"

I looked down at my dreadful elastic-waist shorts. "Sadly, I think there's plenty of room in here."

Mimi laughed. "Finally. A purpose for such a fashion monstrosity." She gave my shoulder a quick squeeze. "Work fast. I don't know how long I can distract him." And then she disappeared from the bathroom.

I dabbed at the tea stain until most of the liquid was absorbed, and then flung the towel in a hamper. Before I left the bathroom, I peeked my head out the door to see if the coast was clear. Then I darted into the room next door and closed the door behind me.

The room was decorated in a traditional blue-and-white theme. The four-poster bed had been draped with thin, gauzy hangings, and the window seat contained enough pillows for a small village. But there in the corner stood the object of my search.

The clothespress was the size of a large chest of drawers. I flung open the doors, but the interior was empty. Nothing but bare wood with no possible hiding places.

Now what?

I wasn't giving up that easily. I ran my hands over the exterior, searching for any possible openings, and that was when I found the hidden door on the side. I swung it open and found six drawers. I jerked open each one, knowing it was futile to hope that the diary would just be sitting there. I examined the drawers for false bottoms, backs, or any other trickery I could think of. Finally I removed every drawer from the clothespress and flipped them over, checking underneath. Nothing. I stared into the yawning hole. The material of the lining was frayed and musty smelling. I ran my hands over it but found nothing there either.

No, no. We couldn't get this close and not find the diary. *Think, Ellen. Think.*

And then I looked up, at the top of the space. Several inches separated the first drawer from the top of the clothespress itself. I ran my hands across the material there, and then I felt it. A tiny catch, like the ones on the back of a picture frame. I found another catch, then a third and a fourth. Each time I turned one, the false top inched downward. I almost wasn't ready when, after I'd turned the fourth one, the panel fell from the hidden compartment into my waiting hands.

I pulled it out and saw the book sitting there on top of the flimsy panel. I blew the dust off the cover. If I hadn't known better, I would have sworn it was Cassandra's diary. But Mrs. Parrot had been right. They were a matched set.

I gently opened the cover to the flyleaf. There, in a very neat hand, was written,

> *Private Property of Miss Jane Austen.*
> *Do Not Read.*
> *That Means You, Cassie.*

 shoved the diary in the back waistband of my shorts, thankful for the forgiving elastic. Then I made my way back to the terrace with as casual an air as I could manage.

Ethan and Daniel rose when I approached the table. "Are you okay?" Ethan asked.

"Yes. Yes, I'm fine. But I think we'd better go. I really do need to change my clothes." I glanced down at the enormous tea stain down the front of my shorts.

"I can leave you my contact information," Daniel said to Ethan, pulling out his wallet and removing a business card. "If you come across anything that might be of interest—"

"I'll be sure to call you."

Mimi rose to her feet. "Ellen, Daniel. Why don't you all head for the pub?" She flashed a smile at Ethan. "We have a taxi waiting there."

"I could have given you a ride—"

"I'd like a private word with Ethan."

I glanced at Daniel. What should we do?

"Mimi—"

"I'm fine. Just a little something that Ethan and I need to clear up."

Ethan looked as if he'd rather have eaten ground glass, but he didn't object.

"We'll wait for you at the pub," Daniel said to Mimi. "If you're sure."

"Quite sure. Now go. Ellen needs to change."

I didn't want to leave Mimi there, but she had a right to some closure with Ethan. "If you're sure," I said, echoing Daniel.

Mimi nodded, and so I didn't have any choice in the matter, really. Jane Austen's diary practically burned my skin where it rested inside the waistband of my shorts. Mimi might have needed closure with Ethan, but I needed to get out of Ethan's house before he figured out what we were up to.

❧❧❧❧❧

"You look like you have something particular to say." Ethan gestured toward the chair where I'd been sitting. "Do make yourself comfortable."

"No, thank you. I'll stand." The girl who had arrived at Oakley Hall on Sunday would never have dreamed of doing what I was about to do, but the girl who stood in Ethan's garden at the end of a very long week was practically a whole new person.

"I want my diary back," I said without preamble.

He didn't flinch. "I don't know what you mean."

"Cassandra's diary. The one I told you about. I don't know how you got into Ellen's hotel room at Langrish, but you must have been very pleased with yourself."

I saw it then, a telltale flicker of an eyelid that betrayed him.

"As I said, I don't know what you mean."

"Look, Ethan, we can do this the easy way, or we can do it the hard way." Clichéd, yes, but it fit the occasion.

He laughed. "Very entertaining, but as I said, I don't have your diary."

"Yes, you do, and you also have the Steventon church key."

I'd figured out that particular piece of the puzzle on the way over in the van. How the key had disappeared about the time he'd moved into the house. How he'd avoided going into the church during the walking tour, so that the warden who was showing us around wouldn't see him.

"You can't prove anything, of course." He was cool as a cucumber.

"I don't think I'll have to prove it. Not once I tell the good folks of Steventon that I saw it here when you gave me the grand tour. I would think that would be enough for a search warrant, or whatever the British equivalent might be."

He blanched. "They'd never believe you."

"They would now that I have Tom and Mrs. Parrot to vouch for me."

I knew, at that moment, that I had won. Ethan's shoulders slumped. "If I give you the diary, you'll leave me alone."

"Completely and totally."

It killed him to do it, I could see, but he disappeared into the house and returned with the book in his hand.

"I had quite high hopes for you, Mimi," he said as he handed it over. "Quite high hopes."

"Sometimes the best hopes are the disappointed ones," I said. "Good-bye, Ethan."

I had never felt so victorious in my life as when I spun on my heel and marched out of that garden. I was half afraid he might change his mind and come after me, so I walked at a brisk pace toward the pub. It wasn't until I was safely inside the Deane Gate Arms, with Tom standing by my side, that my legs turned to water. I slumped against him and looked at Ellen imploringly.

"Please tell me I won't ever have to do anything like that again," I said, and she laughed.

"I promise," she said.

❧❧❧❧❧

Mimi and I had one more stop to make before we left Hampshire. Tom agreed to drive us back to Chawton one last time. Daniel insisted on coming along, and we couldn't exactly leave Mrs. Parrot by the side of the road. So when the van pulled up by the church that stood just outside the gate to Chawton Great

House, I was afraid we would have an audience. But the others seemed to sense that we wanted to be by ourselves. Mimi and I told them that we wanted to visit Cassandra Austen's grave one more time, but I don't think any of the three believed us. At least not entirely.

I carried my tote bag with the box inside. Mimi and I ducked through the covered gate and followed the path around the side of the church. We were concealed from view by the trees and the bulk of the building, but we knew we didn't have much time. While Chawton Great House might not have been open to your average tourist, the churchyard was available to all the visitors from Jane Austen's House Museum just up the road.

Cassandra Austen and her mother were buried along the rear fence. We stood silently by their graves for a long moment. The tombstones looked newer than they should, and I could see that beneath them a pair of older, grayer stones rested flat on the ground. The good folks of Hampshire were not about to let the memory of Jane Austen's family fade.

I reached into my tote bag, withdrew the box, and handed it to Mimi.

She cupped it in her hands. "Is anyone looking?"

I retraced my steps and peeked around the corner of the church, but our only company was several sheep munching grass on the other side of a nearby fence. "The coast is clear," I said, and went back to join her.

The box opened easily under Mimi's hands. "Are you ready?"

"Yes." I reached out so that my hands rested over hers, and together we shook out the contents into the grass at the foot of the graves.

"Rest in peace, Mom," Mimi murmured. A sheep on the other side of the fence let out a long bleat. A gentle breeze stirred the trees and scattered a bit of the ash beyond the Austen graves and across the churchyard.

As soon as the box was empty, Mimi closed it, and I slid it back into my tote.

"So that's it, I guess," she said. It was both appropriate and anticlimactic after all we'd been through.

"Yes. I guess it is," Mimi said.

It seemed strange to turn and leave the only remaining earthly part of my mother among the Austen headstones. At least she would have been happy with our choice, I thought.

☙☙☙☙☙

We headed toward the van, but we'd only gone a few steps when Mrs. Parrot stepped out from the shadows of the side door to the church.

"We're busted," Mimi hissed under her breath, and I tried to keep my expression neutral.

"Just wanted a last look," I said to her, but I could tell she knew exactly what we'd done.

"That was most likely illegal. Or at least should require proper permission from the church authorities."

Mimi and I exchanged guilty glances. Still, it would have been our word against Mrs. Parrot's, and she had no hard evidence. "We have no idea what you're talking about," I said.

Mrs. Parrot cast me a disparaging look. "Badly done, Ellen. I am not a fool."

"No, you're not. But this was a private act that harms no one. I hope that you can leave it at that."

"Actually, it's a decision that concerns me."

I wasn't expecting that response. "In what way?"

Mrs. Parrot leaned heavily on her walking stick. "I'm surprised you haven't guessed the connection. I thought one of you might have by now."

"Connection to what?" Mimi asked in irritation.

"Your connection to me."

The breeze picked up so that it whipped my hair across my face. "We have no connection to you, other than to be thankful for your help with the diary."

"Have you not wondered how I knew about the diary in the first place?" she asked.

"You guessed," I said. "We just confirmed your hunch."

She shook her head. "I haven't told you the whole truth."

"How shocking," Mimi said in a dry tone.

Mrs. Parrot, though, wasn't to be stopped by a little sarcasm. "What do you know of your mother's family?"

That surprised me. "I'm sorry?"

"Your mother's family. What did she tell you about them?"

"She never mentioned them." If Mimi or I ever asked her about her family back in England, she told us that she didn't have any. Her parents were deceased. She had no one left.

"I'm not surprised. We parted on very bad terms."

My head shot up, as did Mimi's. "What do you mean?" she demanded.

Mrs. Parrot took a step toward us and removed her glasses. "We were so close in age that people often mistook us for twins." Her bright blue eyes, as blue as Mimi's, blinked against the sunlight. "I was the oldest, of course. Very much like you, Ellen. Rational. Sensible. While your mother was far more romantic. Like your sister."

"This isn't funny." Mimi's face darkened. "I don't know what game you're playing—"

"No game," Mrs. Parrot said.

I studied her face for a long moment, compared its lines and angles with the fading memory of my mother. The similarities were there, however much I might not want them to be, hidden by age and that profusion of orange hair. But what if this "confession" was simply a ruse to get us to turn over the diaries?

"What was my mother's full name?" I asked her, although anyone with an Internet connection could probably have come up with that information, plus a great deal more.

"Her name was Caroline Anne Dudley. She was born December 16. On Jane Austen's birthday, no less. Her right front tooth had a tiny chip in it. She fell when she was six while we were racing to the village green."

"That doesn't prove anything," Mimi snapped. "Anyone could know those things."

"She had an unusual birthmark on her back," Mrs. Parrot offered. "Almost heart-shaped."

My mouth went dry, and I reached for Mimi's hand. It couldn't be true. It wasn't possible.

"How do we know you didn't just know her from childhood? Any of her friends might have known about the birthmark."

"What can I say that would prove the relationship?" Mrs. Parrot asked. "What could convince you?"

"You could never convince me," Mimi said. "Short of a DNA test, that is."

"That could be arranged." Mrs. Parrot appeared unruffled by the demand.

"You're seriously saying that you're our aunt." I couldn't quite wrap my mind around it, and yet it had the ring of truth. So far on this trip, my instincts had been right about the woman, whether I'd wanted them to be or not.

"Why didn't you say something before?" Mimi's cheeks were flushed with anger. "Very convenient, waiting until now, when it suits your purposes."

Mrs. Parrot assumed an innocent expression. "What purpose could this revelation serve? You have the diaries. I have no reason to lie." She paused, and her shoulders sagged. It was the first sign of weakness in the woman that I'd witnessed all week. She quickly pulled herself together though. "Family can be all too short in supply. I felt that I should tell you. If you choose to make anything of the connection, well . . . that, of course, will be up to you."

I looked at Mimi, and she looked at me, both of us confused. Mrs. Parrot, our aunt? Really?

"Well, I-I," I stammered. "I don't really know what to say."

"You needn't say anything now." Mrs. Parrot tried to appear calm and confident, but I could see from the lines around her mouth that she wasn't as blasé about the whole thing as she appeared.

I reached out and laid a hand on her arm. She almost pulled away, but then stopped herself. "Give us some time," I said as gently as I could. "We've had a lot to take in this past week."

Her other hand covered mine where it rested on her arm. "I understand, my dear. It's just . . . disappointing that you'll both be returning to the States. Time, I'm afraid, is the one thing we don't have."

At the beginning of the week, I would never have thought that I would regret saying good-bye to Mrs. Parrot. Something about her had bothered me from the beginning. As it had turned out, of course, there were a number of reasons why that should have been the case. I was almost beyond being surprised by her revelations anymore. Or anyone else's revelations, for that matter. Secret upon secret. Mine, Mimi's, Daniel's, Mrs. Parrot's. Not to mention Jane and Cassandra Austen's.

"Mrs. Parrot," I said. "There's something I want to show you." I looked at Mimi, and she nodded, understanding instinctively what I was about to do.

I opened my tote bag and pulled out Jane Austen's diary. "Here." I handed it to Mrs. Parrot.

"I was right. They were a matched set." She opened the cover, and I watched her read the inscription on the flyleaf.

"Wait a minute." Mimi reached for the diary, and Mrs. Parrot surrendered it readily. "There's something I want to check." Mimi leafed her way through the pages. "It would be in late November or early December of 1802. Ah, here it is."

"Read it," Mrs. Parrot and I said at the same time, and Mimi did.

> *We fled Manydown like thieves in the night. Cassandra would not speak to me, but Alethea and Elizabeth were most kind. They must know I meant no insult to their brother, only that my own heart is insufficient to the task of releasing Jack Smith. My brother James was quite alarmed to see us so soon returned to Steventon, and I have informed him that Cassandra and I must return to Bath at once. It will be a most tedious journey, since I have sworn never to speak to her again . . .*

> *But that will not last. She meant well enough, as she always does. If only I could be as practical as she, but I am too much a creature of fancy. I cannot marry without love, and neither could Cassie, if it came to it, though she would like to think herself more sensible. She begs my forgiveness, and I extend it, for whatever she has done, 'twas done out of love.*

> *When we return to Bath, I shall begin to revise Elinor and Marianne. I see now that I have got the sisters all wrong. I will have to disguise my characters, of course, make them far more established in their particulars, but Cassie will know. As will I.*

Mimi stopped reading. "So she did base the characters in the book on her and Cassandra."

Mrs. Parrot smiled. "It's been speculated, of course, but never confirmed. This is a major discovery, indeed."

I looked at the diary in Mimi's hands, and I knew one thing for certain. I didn't want the responsibility of it. I was also pretty sure, after everything that had happened, that Mimi wouldn't be interested in selling it.

I took the diary from her and handed it to Mrs. Parrot. "I think you'd better have this."

Mimi didn't protest. "I've had enough of diaries to last me a good long while."

Mrs. Parrot looked at Mimi and then back at me. "You're certain?"

"Absolutely." I mocked wiping my forehead with the back of my hand. "It's a relief to get rid of it."

I did wonder what other treasures of knowledge Jane's diary might hold, but I knew I wasn't the person who should unlock them. I was more than happy to leave that to Mrs. Parrot and the Formidables.

Mimi laughed. "Call it a 'welcome to the family' present."

Just then, Daniel came around the back of the van. "What's so funny?" he asked.

I reached over and took his arm. "It's a long story. I'll tell you on our way to the station." I glanced at my watch. "Come on, or we're going to miss the train."

CHAPTER
TWENTY-SIX

om drove us all to the station at Basingstoke, where we would get a train back to London. I sat beside Daniel in the back of the van. We'd connected on such a deep level, but we hadn't talked about what might happen next. Once we arrived in London, I wondered if we would go our separate ways. All week I'd thought that was what I wanted, but Mimi's lecture in the garden at the Hotel du Vin the night before had helped me to see my life and my choices in a new light. I'd been so busy trying to find perfection that I'd almost missed happiness. In the end, it was an easy trade-off to make. If Daniel would still let me.

He was looking out the window on the other side of the van. I cleared my throat.

"It's been quite a week, hasn't it?" I cringed. Surely I could have found something better than a cliché like that to begin with.

He turned to look at me, and I couldn't tell whether the strange light in his eyes was welcoming or forbidding.

"What have you decided?" he asked. So much for dilly-dallying with clichés.

"I'm not sure how much I get to decide."

He laughed, but he also took my hand. "Ell, the ball's in your court. What happens next is up to you."

"I guess I don't have much experience with calling the shots." The truth of that statement sank in, filtering down through years of being the good daughter, working hard, doing the caretaking. "You'll have to be patient with me. I'm going to make a lot of mistakes."

He threaded his fingers through mine. "As long as we make them together, I think we'll do okay." He raised our hands and kissed my fingers. "I know this probably isn't the happy ending you've dreamed of all your life. It's not like an Austen novel."

"Actually," I said. "It is." One day soon, I would ask for more details about his life with Melissa, and I would meet his daughters. But for now, I had learned that I needed to write my own story, thanks to Cassandra and Jane. They had made the best out of the circumstances life had dictated to them, and I could do a lot worse than to follow in their footsteps.

"I want you to meet my girls," Daniel said, echoing my thoughts.

Tears stung my eyes. "I want that too." One door was closing in my life, but another was opening. It was up to me to walk through it. This time, though, I knew I'd have Daniel at my side. I would also have my sister.

❦❦❦❦❦

Ellen was in the back, talking to Daniel, and I sat beside Tom in the front seat, a bundle of nerves. He shot me a measuring look. "Having second thoughts?"

I shook my head. "Just dreading telling Ellen that I won't be flying home with her."

He reached over and patted my knee. "She'll understand." He glanced in the rearview mirror. "Besides, I think her focus may be on other things very shortly."

I resisted the urge to turn around and see what he meant, but I could guess. Ellen had taken my advice.

Basingstoke bustled with traffic and had more roundabouts than anyplace on earth. We finally made it to the station, and Tom parked the van just outside the entrance.

"I'll get the luggage," he said to the others, and I knew the time had come. I walked over to Ellen and linked my arm through hers.

"I need to talk to you."

She looked at me, surprised. "What's wrong?"

There was nothing else to do but just say it. "I'm not going back to London with you. I'm staying here."

"What do you mean you're staying here? As in England 'staying here?'" Her arm went rigid.

I nodded. I'd known she wouldn't like it, and there was no way I was going to convince her I wasn't being ridiculously impulsive. The only saving grace was that she did like Tom.

"What about New York?" she asked with a glance toward the van, where Tom was wrangling the luggage. "How can you change your mind about something like that? You've wanted that your whole life."

"Um, Ell, not to be a smart aleck, but that's a little bit like the pot asking the kettle why it's black." I shot a glance at Daniel, who was standing nearby, waiting for us.

Her mouth fell open. "That's different."

"How?"

"Because it just is, that's all."

"A well-formulated argument." I smiled. I couldn't help myself. "I think we've both come to see that it's time to let go of old dreams. Time to come up with some new ones."

"But it's so far away."

That was her real objection, I knew, and it was my biggest regret. Finally, after all these years, we'd managed to establish a bond as sisters, and now we were going to be farther apart than ever, geographically speaking.

"We can Skype," I said.

"I don't even know what that is."

"Video chat. Over the Internet. Besides"—I put my arm around her—"won't you be moving away from Dallas to be with Daniel?"

She looked surprised. "Well, I guess so . . . "

"Aw, c'mon, Ell. Didn't it occur to you that you and Daniel would have to live in the same city? And I don't see him giving up a well-established business."

"There will be an ocean between us." She looked so forlorn, and I felt the same way.

"An ocean, we can transcend. Not speaking to each other, that's the really big divide we've overcome."

She started to cry in earnest, sniffling and wiping at her tears. "When did you get to be the wise one?"

I glanced at my watch. "About five minutes ago, I think."

I loved the smile that spread across her face. "I think Jane Austen would appreciate the irony of all this."

"I know. Mom would too. She turned us into the Dashwood sisters after all."

"So you're really staying? With Tom?"

"I'll get a job in a shop or something for now, so he and I can have a chance to get to know each other. Mom's estate gives me a little cushion. We'll see what happens from there."

Daniel walked over to us, rolling Ellen's little suitcase, and I gave him a fierce hug. "Take care of her. I mean it."

He looked at me in confusion. "You're not going?"

I laughed. "Ellen will explain it to you on the train."

Ellen had stepped away and was talking to Mrs. Parrot. I walked up to them and reached inside my handbag to retrieve Cassandra's diary. Then I turned to Mrs. Parrot and held the book out to her. "Ellen gave you Jane's diary, and I'm going to do the same with Cassandra's."

Her eyebrows shot up. "Are you sure?"

I didn't have to look at my sister to know that she agreed with my decision. "I think they should both be with the Formidables."

Ellen frowned. "Mimi—"

"It's okay, Ell. I know this is the right thing to do." The Austen sisters had given something to Ellen and me far more precious than a valuable diary or two. I was only returning the favor.

"Thank you." Mrs. Parrot looked pleased and touched, as well as a little vulnerable. I'd never thought I would see that. She paused and then cleared her throat. "But I have consulted with the membership committee, Mimi, and we should like you to be the keeper of Cassandra's diary."

"What?" I couldn't believe it when Mrs. Parrot pressed the book back into my hands.

She nodded to Ellen. "We would ask you as well, my dear, to safeguard Jane's, but we have strict requirements that any member must be a resident of the United Kingdom. Since your sister has elected to stay—"

"I understand." Ellen looked at me with the funniest smile on her face. "Somehow it seems fitting."

I looked down at the book in my hand in astonishment. "But if I have this, it means . . . "

"That you are the newest Formidable. There will be some paperwork, and the matter of meeting one or two of the others. But as your mother was well known to many of them . . . "

I looked at Mrs. Parrot and tried not to let my jaw hang open. "Me? A Formidable?"

She chuckled. "You always were, my dear. You just didn't know it."

❧❧❧❧❧

A week ago, I would never have imagined the good-bye scene that Mimi and I enacted in front of the Basingstoke train station. The ferocity of the hug, the copiousness of the tears, the men waiting patiently for us to finish our lengthy farewell.

All along, we had been looking for the wrong thing. We thought we were supposed to unearth some big secret between the sisters, but it had never been about the secrets that Jane and Cassandra Austen kept *from* each other. It was about the secrets they kept *for* each other, from the world. I wanted to say that to Mimi, but instead I just hugged her.

"Mom outsmarted us," I whispered in Mimi's ear, laughing and crying at the same time.

"Yes, she did." If she had hugged me any tighter, I wouldn't have been able to breathe. But I didn't care.

We couldn't have been more pleased for our mother to be right.

About the Author

Beth Pattillo's love for Jane Austen was born when she studied at Westfield College, University of London, for one glorious semester. Her passion quickly became an obsession, necessitating regular trips to Enland over the past twenty years. Her most recent journey included a Hampshire pilgrimage to visit many of the sites included in this book. When not dreaming of life "across the pond," Beth lives in Nashville, Tennessee, with her husband and two children.